VWK
VAMPIRE WARRIOR KINGS

**HE'S HER NIGHTMARE...
AND HER FANTASY...**

Seduced by the Vampire KING

NEW YORK TIMES BESTSELLER

LAURA KAYE

Seduced by the Vampire KING

VWK
VAMPIRE WARRIOR KINGS

NEW YORK TIMES BESTSELLER
LAURA KAYE

SEDUCED BY THE VAMPIRE KING

SECOND EDITION March 2020

FIRST EDITION June 2012

SEDUCED BY THE VAMPIRE KING © Laura Kaye.

ALL RIGHTS RESERVED.

No part or whole of this book may be used, reproduced, distributed, or transmitted in any manner whatsoever without written permission of the author except in the case of brief quotations embodied in critical articles or reviews. The unauthorized reproduction or distribution of this copyrighted work via electronic or mechanical means is a violation of international copyright law and subjects the violator to severe fines and/or imprisonment. If you are reading the ebook, it is licensed for your personal enjoyment only. The ebook may not be re-sold or given away to other people. If you would like to share the ebook, please purchase an additional copy for each person you share it with. Please do not participate in piracy of copyrighted materials in violation of the author's rights. Thank you for respecting the author's work.

The characters and events portrayed in this book are fictional and/or are used fictitiously and are solely the product of the author's imagination. Any similarity to persons living or dead, places, businesses, events, or locales is purely coincidental.

Cover Design by Kim Killion

THE VAMPIRE WARRIOR KINGS SERIES

IN THE SERVICE OF THE KING
SEDUCED BY THE VAMPIRE KING
TAKEN BY THE VAMPIRE KING

CHAPTER 1

Nikolai Vasilyev was right in the middle of the shit, and it was exactly where he wanted to be.

Shots erupted from two positions ahead of him and ricocheted off the abandoned cinder-block streetscape he'd been patrolling. Ducking into an alley, he felt a telltale whiz of air buzzing his ear and went flat against the concrete wall of the old factory. The frigid winter night air burned Nikolai's lungs. His hackles rose and his fangs stretched out. His enemies were close enough he could feel their evil.

He wanted trouble. And he found it. Or it found him. Semantics.

Somewhere ahead, concealed among the long-neglected buildings, a band of Soul Eaters apparently had a sniper's roost. Those demented murderers jeopardized the hidden vampire world by caving in to the lure of exsanguination. All vampires drank from humans, but only the Soul Eaters consumed human souls by drinking through the last beat of their hearts, then removing and eating it. Their addictive recklessness threatened to expose them all to the broader human world, and escalated the ancient war between the two rival strains of immortals.

Nikolai plotted out a plan of attack, the street taking shape in his mind's eye like a 3-D simulator. Dark satisfaction pooled in his gut. Sending these little birdies flying from their nest—permanently—was going to turn this night from a miserable waste to decently tolerable. It didn't get any better than that for him.

Not anymore.

Not since he'd dishonored himself, and the Soul Eaters killed Evgeny and Kyril.

The hushed, efficient chatter of his warriors sounded in his earpiece and drew Nikolai from his thoughts. Torturing himself over his brothers' deaths had no place out on the street. There was plenty of time for that while the sun kept him inside cooling his heels.

He peeked over his shoulder and around the corner of the building. A volley of shots rang out and Nikolai growled a curse under his breath, his gaze swinging around to the rusted industrial street lamp illuminating his position. He sighted the bulb and squeezed off a single bullet that solved that problem, then turned, fell to a crouch and took another light out farther down the street.

"Who's got a lock on that gunfire?" came Mikhail's voice through the earbud. His second-in-command was a consummate soldier and the only thing holding his kingdom together at the moment. Nikolai was man enough to admit that. "Report in."

One by one, six of his finest warriors gave the all clear and confirmed their locations.

Nikolai sighed. He didn't want to share this one. He didn't want to have to rein himself in. When he found the Soul Eaters' position, he wanted to unleash the inhuman monster within, to surrender to the grief and rage boiling inside him as he tore his enemies to pieces with his bare hands and fangs. No fucking audience required.

As if they all didn't worry about him enough. He hated the weighted silences and sidelong glances that seemed to follow him wherever he went these days. Christ, he needed to release a little of the volcanic agony expanding in his chest, making it hard to breathe, hard to think. Hard to care.

An awkward silence passed before he heard, "My lord, what's your area of operation?" Mikhail's tone no doubt sounded level and professional to everyone else, but Nikolai recognized the wariness and exhaustion in his oldest friend's voice. Guilt soured his gut. "I say again, my lord, what's your AO?"

Focusing on the task at hand, and not the way he was failing Mikhail—hell, failing all of them—Nikolai did a quick ammunition check and ran through his mental plan one more time. He took a deep calming breath and centered himself, using his memory of the last time he saw his brothers, expressions frozen in death, to fuel his resolve.

"Son of a bitch, Nikolai, answer me. You're there, aren't you?"

With indecipherable words still ranting from the speaker, Nikolai tugged the unit from his ear and yanked it from around his neck. He dropped it to the ground and crushed the receiver with his boot, insuring no one could come behind him and eavesdrop on his warriors' movements.

With an apology to Mikhail and a vow to Evgeny and Kyril, Nikolai moved out onto the street, staying low and tight to the building. He set his sights on the general location from which the earlier shots seemed to originate and ducked into doorways and alleys whenever he could. Twenty meters ahead, a third street lamp posed an insurmountable problem. Whether he got rid of it or left it intact, he would reveal his position to the enemy.

He voted for the cover of darkness and took it out with a single shot, only the sudden blackness and sprinkling of glass against the concrete sidewalk revealing what he'd done.

It was enough.

A barrage of gunfire erupted, the snaps and crackles of high-speed projectiles close enough to make him dive for cover. The enemy fire brought something useful with it, too—the Soul Eaters' muzzle flashes gave away their position and told Nikolai precisely where he needed to go.

Release and relief were so fucking close.

The break in the gunfire meant they'd likely lost his position in the dark, so he bolted from his place behind a car and flashed across the street at preternatural speed. Closer now. He was so close he could smell their fear. He reveled in it. Drank it down into his belly like the sweetest nectar. Soon, he would gorge himself on it.

Reconnoitering the new side of the street, Nikolai shoved out of his hiding place and darted across the intersection to the block that housed the Soul Eaters' fortified position.

Victory lured him forward, out into the open.

Bullets rained down around him, but he ducked and twisted, plowing onward. His fangs pinched his bottom lip as he hauled ass to safety. A doorway loomed ahead, one that should be shielded from the nest above.

A new barrage of gunfire clattered and echoed in the space between the wasted buildings. The sound hurt his head and disoriented him. Nikolai couldn't place its location.

And then searing fire tore into his shoulder, the side of his neck, the back of his thigh.

Fuck, somehow they'd gotten behind him. And no one was covering his six.

Because he hadn't let them.

He was hit. Hit bad.

Howling more from the agony of defeat than the pain of the tainted bullets, poisoned with the blood of the dead, Nikolai flashed down the side street before the blood loss and infection drained his powers, his life. He pushed himself to keeping moving and lost track of the distance he covered as he retreated from the abandoned industrial quarter toward the general direction of Moscow's city center.

His breathing was loud in his own ears, a mix of a rasp and a gurgle that told him the neck wound was critical.

Son of a bitch. Mikhail was going to kill him. Assuming he survived.

The poison hit his heart as the industrial area gave way to apartment buildings and shops. He crashed against the brick wall of a building and his vision blurred and twisted. The world went sideways and he hit the ground so hard it rattled his brain in his skull. Between the blood loss and the poison, moving took herculean effort, but he had to get off the street.

Gun still tight in his grip, he dragged himself on his forearms, pulling the dead weight of his body toward a gravel path that ran alongside the building. His muscles screamed, sweat stung his eyes, and his gasping breath scorched his throat. A thirst more intense than any he'd ever felt made his tongue feel thick and his fangs ache.

As the building's shadow covered him, Nikolai could move no more. He hoped the kingdom he'd refused to lead these long months would survive the succession crisis his death would leave behind.

Regrets. Oh, so many regrets.

Bitter cold bent his bones until he was sure they would snap. He shivered, sending his teeth and fangs clattering against one another.

How wonderful it would be to have the warmth and companionship of a mate right now.

He had not strength enough to even chide himself for the thought.

A black fog descended, stealing first his sight, then his hearing. Tortured thoughts remained to the end until, mercifully, they too faded to nothing.

Just like him.

CHAPTER 2

VWK

One question kept repeating itself in Kate Bordessa's mind: *What the hell am I doing here?*

She stuffed her gloved hands in the pockets of her parka and ducked her face against the cold night air. It was one-thirty in the morning and the street was empty, except for her.

Unanswered questions and a sense of anxiety had kept her awake until she'd finally given up on sleep, thrown on some clothes, and hopped the underground metro at the university. She thought walking around Red Square and seeing the cathedrals, palaces, and towers there would cheer her, would remind her why she had come to study in Moscow. But not even the vivid colors of Saint Basil's or the festively lit outline of the GUM department store had made her feel any less like something wasn't right.

So she'd walked, hoping physical fatigue would drive away the unfounded anxiety.

Though she remained firm on the reason she'd fled the States—her parents wanted a destiny for her she could never accept—Kate couldn't escape the restlessness that always left her feeling she wasn't doing something she was supposed to be doing. Under the surface, a sense of unease, as if she'd forgotten an important appointment or a commitment, nagged at her. In quiet moments, a gloom of foreboding descended over her, setting her heart to racing and making her momentarily sure some tragedy had unfurled.

And *she* might've stopped it.

It was all making her crazy. And homesick. Maybe it was her looming birthday that was causing her unease. Though you wouldn't think turning twenty-one would be traumatic.

Pausing at an intersection, Kate swept her gaze in a circle around her. The can of mace in her pocket boosted her confidence to be out here, but a woman still had to stay aware of her surroundings. Finally, the light changed and she tugged her hood snug to her face as she crossed the street.

Shops, businesses and office buildings gave way to apartment buildings. She didn't know this neighborhood well, but she was familiar enough with the city after living here for five months to be certain if she kept going a few blocks, she'd come to a metro stop on the line she needed. Hell, maybe she'd even pass the closest one and keep walking until the one after.

A couple tucked against each other passed her on the sidewalk. Their low voices and laughter heightened her loneliness, unleashing a deep-seated fear she'd never find that sense of belonging others seemed to develop so effortlessly.

It was as if she was a square peg in the round hole of life. Never had a boyfriend. Barely been kissed. Parents urging her to join them in something she couldn't fathom. And the closer it got to her birthday next Friday, the more acute all these confusing, ridiculous feelings became.

It was almost as if a clock was ticking down to…something? What, she just didn't know.

Suddenly, her scalp prickled and the hair on her neck and arms rose. Her stomach clenched and flip-flopped. What the hell?

Sure someone was stalking her, Kate shook her hood off and whirled, but the street was empty. Still, the ominous feeling was so convincing, it took every ounce of willpower to restrain her desire to run..

Finally, she stopped trying to resist, and broke out into a jog, relief flooding into her when the squat red M of the metro came into view up ahead. Gloved hand grasping the mace, she passed one apartment building, then another,.

"Shit." Her ankle twisted off the edge of a broken curb she hadn't noticed. Thankfully, the height of her boot prevented her from rolling it enough to cause a sprain. Damn thing still hurt, though. She paused and leaned a hand against the corner of the building, her exhalations fogging on the cold air.

Take a freaking breath, Kate.

She rotated her foot and stretched her ankle, reassuring herself it was fine. She just needed to go home and go to bed. Everything would look better in the morning.

The breeze kicked up and Kate froze.

What was that smell? Something spicy and warm. She couldn't begin to place it, but all at once she forgot her panic. Swallowing the saliva pooling on her tongue, she inhaled more of that enticing smell like a lioness scenting the most delicious meal on the wind. She looked up at the apartments, but everything was dark. Behind her, the street remained empty. To her left, a driveway disappeared into darkness...

And the darkness concealed the source of that scent.

She wasn't sure how she knew it, but she did.

One step. Another. Lured into the darkness. By something that called to her very soul, that appealed to her on a primal level.

She had to...what? She wasn't sure. Find it? See it?

Taste it.

The urges were so instinctual she didn't even think about questioning them.

Shaking off the odd haze, Kate removed her smartphone from her jeans pocket and woke up the screen to provide a bit of light. A series of selections turned on the phone's flashlight, which cast a brighter, broader illumination.

Boots. The first thing she saw was a pair of big black boots.

She gasped so hard and unexpectedly, the cold hurt her throat.

The man attached to those boots was huge, unmoving, and facedown in the dirt and stones of the driveway.

Without question, he was the source of the scent.

The sensation of alarm returned, stronger than before. Not out of fear for herself, but out of fear for him.

She had the oddest sensation of being sucked through a tunnel, or of seeing her life replayed in fast-forward behind her eyes. And, either way, the end led her here.

To this moment. To this alley. To this man.

Weeks and months of foreboding and worry and dread all culminated right here. Her certainty was so fundamental, so intense, that she knew it the same way she knew her name, or that the grass was green.

Pomogite mne. Help me.

At the sound of the distant voice, Kate spun, wielding her flashlight phone like a weapon and shining the light around. "Who's there?"

But the alley was otherwise empty. Rushing to the corner of the building, she found the street clear, too.

Trembling, she cut the glow back to the man and scanned his body with it. Blood soaked through the dark fabric of his pants on his right thigh. A lot of blood. A hole tore through his coat near his right shoulder. Long strands of brown hair peeked out from underneath a black knit cap.

She stepped to the other side of him, the dull ache of her ankle forgotten, and crouched near his head. Her light shined on the side of his face, but between his position and the cap she couldn't make out much except… "Oh, shit."

Blood coated the scruff on his jaw, his neck, and the arm he'd collapsed on, and it had dripped to the ground beneath him, not soaking in but pooling on the frozen surface. Heart in her throat, she gingerly peeled back the lapel of his coat. Her stomach turned. His neck was literally torn apart.

Thoughts shot through her brain in a rapid-fire barrage. *Is he alive? Oh, God, he's gotta be dead. Could the shooter still be here? That blood…that freaking blood is what I smell. But how? Help him. Help him!*

Kate dialed 03 on her phone and waited, eyes still on the man's form, trying to discern movement. Gently, she laid her hand on the middle of his back. There! Her hand felt the soft rise and fall her eyes couldn't perceive.

Relief rushed through her.

The operator answered and briskly inquired about the nature of her emergency and her location, and Kate had never been more glad for her fluency in Russian. "I found an unconscious man. I think he's been shot. He's bleeding really badly from his neck and leg."

"Did you see the shooting? Is the shooter still in the area?"

She whipped her gaze to the right, then the left. All remained silent and still, except her. But what if whoever did this was hiding? Watching her. Watching him.

Rage shot up Kate's spine, almost stealing her breath. She was nearly disoriented by the emotion's intensity and unexpectedness. *No one will hurt him again.* Dizziness threatened at the bizarre thought.

She shook her head and struggled to be present in the moment. "Uh, no. I...I didn't see anything. And I don't think anyone else is here."

The dispatcher fired off a stream of questions Kate did her best to answer. At the woman's suggestion, she yanked off a glove and sacrificed it to the cause of applying pressure to his neck wound.

Anything to help him.

She turned down the offer to stay on the line until the ambulance arrived. The flashlight feature drained her cell battery quickly and it was already running low.

Nuzhna pomoshch! Need help.

Kate fumbled her cell phone at the reappearance of the

voice. Her nerves were just frayed. That's what it was. Must be. There was no one else here.

She set her phone on the ground next to them, light shining where she was working on his neck, and blew out a breath that failed to calm. "Come on, mister. Hang in there. Help's on its way."

Blood saturated her glove and Kate gasped as the warmth kissed her palm. She jerked back and scrubbed her right hand against her thigh. The oddest tingling erupted in her other hand as she rubbed against the denim. Ignoring the sensation, Kate tossed the ruined glove away and pulled off her left one. Her gaze scanned him as she murmured in low tones for him to hold on.

His hat. His hat was thicker than her glove. Gently, she pulled the cap off the back of his head, spilling longish brown hair. She slid her palm under his forehead to provide some cushion against the cold hard ground as she removed the front of the hat. Securing the thick folded knit against the crook of his neck, she eased her hand out from under him.

His head rolled enough to reveal his face in profile.

Kate gaped and moaned.

She scrabbled backward until her spine slammed into the brick wall of the looming building.

Between his parted, anguished lips, two sharp teeth protruded.

Fangs.

He had fangs.

CHAPTER 3

VWK

Vampire.
 Her heart pounded in her chest, forcing her blood through her veins so hard and fast the roaring whoosh of it filled her ears.

He was a freaking vampire!

But…*oh, God*…what kind?

Kate had to look. Either way, she had to know what she was dealing with. Light-headedness threatened from her rapid breathing, but Kate forced herself to creep onto her knees and reach out a shaking hand. Shining her flashlight on his face, she flinched as her thumb pressed to his eyelid.

Please, please, please.

The light quivered as she lifted the thin membrane of skin, hoping against hope it didn't reveal the soulless black iris and sclera of a Soul Eater. Her whole body sagged in relief. A perfectly white sclera and bright sapphire-blue iris shined out at her.

Oh, thank God.

Not one of the evil ones, then. She dropped her head

into her hands and sucked in deep breaths that did little to ease her.

She'd traveled five thousand miles to get away from vampires—from studying them, preparing to serve them, from the possibility of a future involving them—and here she sat, in a pitch-black alley, with an unconscious one at her feet.

And, *holy shit*, she wasn't even going to let herself think about why the vampire's blood had affected her that way. Why it still affected her body and instincts and reactions even now.

But damnit if everything she'd been running from hadn't just caught up to her.

Her parents were members of the Electorate, a group of influential humans who knew about the presence of vampires in the world, hid their existence, and worked with them in their fight against evil vampires known as Soul Eaters. For their efforts, the humans reaped benefits from the alliance—including earning the vampires' protection and access to their blood, which cured disease and slowed the aging process significantly.

When she'd turned sixteen, Kate's parents had shared their secret and encouraged her to enroll in a program that would immerse her in the history and culture of vampires, preparing her to one day take their place on the Electorate Council. The program also entered her in a training class to become what they called a Proffered, a virgin human woman trained to serve the blood needs of the vampire warrior class—and possibly become a lifelong mate. Apparently, all vampires were born male, so the perpetuation of their species could only be achieved through the joining of the races, a joining that cemented their alliance through kin ties and not just diplomacy alone.

In the beginning, Kate had been a lot curious and at least a little interested, even if it was also equally scary as hell. Still, she loved medieval history and was intrigued by her discovery of this world within a world. Her parents' enthusiasm and pride also drove her. And, as she learned of her parents' prominence within the Council, she felt the weight of familial obligation, too. But the whole Proffered thing…it always scared her as much as it fascinated her.

The idea of it felt…objectifying and exploitative.

When she gave someone her virginity, she wanted it to be because they liked and cared for her—she didn't even have to have full-out love. But she certainly didn't want it to be because she happened to have the ability to fulfill some biological need. And the idea of becoming a vampire's lifelong mate—what did that even mean?

The whole thing raised so many questions.

So, as she'd neared her twentieth birthday—the year in which human blood apparently became particularly powerful for a vampire—she'd known she would never be able to go through with it, and she'd withdrawn from her training early.

She stared at the man—the *warrior*, probably—in front of her and had to admit, despite her jaw-dropping surprise at encountering the very thing she'd believed she could never accept, that a fierce strain of protectiveness flowed through her.

She gasped. The ambulance! The ambulance would be here soon. *Oh, my God. They can't find him.*

Kate flew upright, her back ramrod straight. She might

not want to become a vampire's mate, but that didn't mean she had any intention of revealing their existence to the broader world. Between her training and her family, she understood very well how important the good vampires were to humans' survival against the evil ones, and thus how vital it was to keep the secret.

They had to get out of here. She had to get them out.

Though she'd never seen it firsthand, she'd learned vampires could heal, so her concerns about moving him alleviated a little. But she couldn't even attempt it while he remained facedown.

Silently apologizing, she braced both hands on the shoulder closest to the neck wound and entry hole in the back of his coat. Digging the toes of her boots into the gravel, it took all her strength to get him moving, but finally she rolled him onto his back. Pulse racing, her gaze raked over his features, but they were hard to make out through the dark and the loose strands of hair and smears of dirt and blood that covered his face.

She frowned. The left side of his hair bore no braid. Not a warrior after all, then, as braids represented the fraternity and bond of the warrior class.

Her thoughts scattered as her eyes caught a glint of metal on his chest. His bloody hand gripped a gun, a semi-automatic SIG Sauer, if she wasn't mistaken. Some introductory weapons training had been her father's idea.

Frowning, she inhaled a deep breath and reached for it, surprised at how much effort it took to pry his fingers free from the grip. "If you can hear me, I'm not stealing it, I promise. I'm just going to hold it for you. I don't want to try to move you with it loose."

A growl sounded in her head. Her gaze flashed to his unconscious face. The voice she'd heard, this sound—could they be coming from him? She'd never learned of such a thing, although she'd also never before met a real living breathing vampire—or wanted to.

"We have to get you out of here," she said in a hushed voice. "Please."

His fingers relaxed. Or so it seemed. She finally pulled the weapon free.

With the help of her flashlight, she engaged the decocking mechanism on the side of the gun's frame, making it safe to stow. But it was too big for her coat pocket. Feeling ridiculous, she holstered it in the waistband on the back of her jeans, grimacing at the feeling of the cold metal digging into her skin.

Stepping to his shoulders, Kate reached under his arms and gripped the fabric there. Her hands were so cold that she had to fight for purchase against the material. She rose into a crouched position and tugged.

Nothing. Not even a budge. Oh, no. "Come on, mister. We have to go before the ambulance gets here."

This time she tried hooking her arms under his, and that worked, but it placed so much strain on her back she had to keep pausing. Thank God the authorities moved slowly in Moscow. Her ears strained to hear the far-off sound of sirens that would tell her she was out of time.

As she dragged him in uneven starts and stops over the gravel, her hunched-over position brought her face close to his. A warm thrill zinged down her spine and settled into her stomach like a shot of vodka. His spicy scent was so strong and appealing up close she had to resist leaning in farther, pressing her nose to his cheek, his hair.

His throat.

Jeez, Kate, get your freaking head together.

They rounded the back of the building and victory flared in her gut. Now to find a place to conceal him while the ambulance came and went. Kate straightened to a standing position and pressed her palms into her lower back, stretching and soothing. A street lamp on the other side of the building's rear revealed a small parking lot with a half-dozen cars parked against a chain-link fence and a Dumpster close to where she stood. Maybe she could hide him behind the line of cars. Maybe the ambulance crew would assume it was a false report. Maybe they wouldn't see the disturbed gravel where she'd dragged him.

That was a lot of damn maybes, but what else could she do?

"We're almost there, now," she murmured as she bent again and hooked her arms under his. "Hold on." Pushing herself harder, she tugged him toward the row of cars. But what was she going to do with him after this crisis passed?

She shook her head and focused on pulling him. She could only worry about one thing at a time.

A wet, throaty groan sounded from the vampire.

Kate's gaze dropped to his face, only dimly illuminated by the distant light. "It's all right," she said. "You're gonna be all right."

Her foot went down farther than she expected. Kate stumbled, her boot wedged in some kind of hole, and struggled to hold her balance. She failed.

She landed so hard her breath exploded out of her. The

way she'd had her arms wedged under his kept them hooked together, and the vampire's dead weight landed on her aching legs.

Her tailbone throbbing from the impact with the ground and the way the gun's barrel dug into her skin, Kate groaned and fought to pull herself free of him.

Another, louder growl rolled out of his chest, like the low rumble of thunder, and he stirred, his head jerking against her thighs.

If he regained consciousness, this would be so much easier. "Hey, are you—"

A tearing pain ripped into her wrist.

Kate cried out and tried to wrench away, but— *Oh, my God! He bit me!* She gasped and moaned, "No!"

She threw every muscle into escaping the iron grip of his hands on her forearm and his impaling fangs in her radial artery. Her boots scrambled for purchase against the loose gravel but his weight held her down. With her free hand, she grabbed a fistful of brown hair and yanked.

The sound that ripped from his throat issued an animalistic warning her body recognized. Her heart raced in her chest, her scalp prickled and the hair rose on her arms and neck. Clutching her arm, he rolled onto his side and settled most of his big body within the cradle of her thighs, one shoulder pinning her hips tight and hard.

Pozhaluĭsta, pozhaluĭsta. Please, he begged over and over, wearing down her resistance as his tone became more desperate.

Blood rushing behind her ears, the sound even louder for the deep, sucking draws exiting through her wrist, Kate went still.

Please, he groaned in her head. *Dying.*

The abject need in his voice sucker punched her. Her hand slackened in his thick hair, but didn't fall away altogether.

Dying.

The possibility made her feel dizzy and weak. Or maybe that was just the blood loss.

For sure, though, injured as he was, he must require a lot of blood. Could she really deny him what he needed to survive? Did she even want to? His tongue laved over her skin, and her body knew the answer even if her brain resisted.

As she acquiesced, the hard metal digging into her sacrum captured her attention. The gun. Kate debated and rejected the idea in the blink of an eye. He was one of the good ones. And he wouldn't kill her. As soon as the thought passed through her brain, her heart knew the truth of it.

I give…my word.

His being in her head felt inexplicably right. She sagged where she was half lying against the ground and gave in to his desire.

He unleashed an anguished whimper. *Thank you.*

Kate sucked in a breath at the way he seemed to respond to her thoughts. Without conscious thought, she stroked his hair and turned her head to watch him. The darkness and the angle of his face concealed the feeding, but Kate didn't need to see it.

She felt it. In every cell of her body.

CHAPTER 4

The more Kate gave in to his need, the more she perceived the movement of blood where they were joined. And the longer he sucked the lifeblood from her, the more she became almost inebriated with the feeling of his hands and tongue and fangs on her. In her.

Arousal spiked through her body, hot and unexpected.

Kate arched under him. Her fingers tightened in his hair, but not as before. This time, her grip encouraged and embraced him. A moan tore up her throat. She wasn't even sure what she needed, she simply knew her body yearned for something more.

From him. With him.

What was happening to her?

A big hand squeezed her hip and Kate jolted at the pressure. He shifted his position again, bringing the weight of his chest hard against the increasingly sensitive nerves at the junction of her thighs.

She thrust her hips upward, helpless to resist her body's

growing need. The heat between her legs was all the more noticeable for the cold air surrounding them. But the longer he fed, the hotter she got, as if there was a cocoon surrounding and protecting them.

All Kate could feel, all she knew, was the two of them intertwined in a moment more intimate than any she'd ever experienced.

Over the sound of her panting breaths and his wet sucking, she swore she could almost hear something like purring, a low growl of deep satisfaction. The soft rumble added to the electricity building between her legs.

Around her, the world spun until it blurred. Within her, a white-hot energy pooled low in her belly. Never, ever had her body threatened to go to pieces this fast. It was as if his very presence had flipped a switch inside her. He shifted between her legs again.

Oh, God. Oh, God, if he didn't stop, she was going to explode.

Was this what it was always like to be bitten by a vampire?

He whimpered, trembled. Kate shook off the heavy haze of her arousal and forced herself to lean up onto an elbow. His head shook on his shoulders, as though he struggled to hold it upright.

She remembered the shredded appearance of his neck and winced in sympathy. "You could—" Kate swallowed thickly "—let me sit up and lay with your head in my lap. It'll be easier for you that way."

His mouth stilled against her, but didn't release.

"It's not a trick," she said. Kate pushed herself into an awkward sitting position, and the vampire moved ungracefully to allow her. His head lolled back onto her thigh, one hand still forming a manacle around her arm. She looked down into his face, burning with the desire to see him more clearly. His eyelids fluttered and sagged as if they were too heavy to lift, and ultimately fell closed.

When she was as settled as she could be with him sprawled over her legs and lying in her lap, she stroked his forehead back over his messy hair. "Okay, just hurry. You need to get out of here. And leave me some."

His mouth and tongue moved languorously against her skin. The sensation ricocheted up her arm and through every vein, spiking heat throughout her whole body.

My guardian angel, he intoned in solemn Russian in what she now knew without question was his voice.

Her heart squeezed at the reverence of his thought. "Well, I don't know about— Oh, shit." Warmth flooded over her thigh. His blood. His neck seemed to leak as fast as he drank. Icy fear snaked down her spine. "You're bleeding really badly."

Her gloves and his cap were long gone.

Kate only had one thing left: she unzipped her parka and shrugged it off her free arm. Frigid air flooded into the bubble of warmth she'd imagined surrounded them and made it hard to breathe.

A scuff, from the far end of the alley.

Kate froze and tilted her head, listening.

It sounded like… Her ears strained. Footsteps?

Fear erupted in her gut. Couldn't be the ambulance. There had been no sirens. No vehicle noise. And why would the paramedics be so purposely quiet?

Brilliant red rage displaced the fear and set her senses on high alert.

All her calm disappeared and morphed into stone-cold protectiveness and fierce possessiveness. *He is mine. No one will take him.*

Operating on instinct, Kate's hand found and removed the SIG from her jeans, a dark satisfaction flooding her as she returned the decocking lever to its live position. She was so damn glad he'd gone for her left wrist, leaving her dominant hand free to shoot. If necessary.

Holding the gun out over his body, she aimed for the darkness of the driveway. Her heart lodged in her throat, but her hand held steady.

Three hulking shapes stepped into the dim light behind the building.

"Jesus, we found him," one of them said.

"Fuck. The human's armed," another called.

Before she'd even blinked, they'd disappeared. "Drop your weapon," a deep male voice barked.

As if. She whispered, "You have to wake up now, vampire. There are others here. And I don't know if they're friend or foe. Please. Wake up."

"Drop your weapon," the unseen man barked again. "Last chance."

"No way. Leave us alone. We're not your business," she said with more bravado than she felt.

"The hell you're not—"

"Enough," someone commanded. "I'm coming out," the same voice continued. "And I'm unarmed." Hands raised, a figure stepped where she could see him.

The man—the vampire, she assumed—was huge. Same

dark paramilitary dress and black cap as her vampire wore. Didn't mean they were on the same side, though.

He pointed with his chin. "He's hurt."

Kate glared at him, refusing to be distracted. Her shooting hand remained ready. She had no idea how she was going to get them out of this.

"I'm Mikhail."

"I don't want to shoot you, but I will." Her voice had none of the shakiness she felt in her gut.

He nodded. "Won't you put the gun down so we can talk about how to help him?" he asked in accented English.

Her vampire's sucking pulls slowed against her wrist. He groaned and his mouth went slack.

Kate wanted nothing more than to divert her gaze and check on him, assure herself he was still breathing. For the first time, her hand trembled around the gun. Over her frozen cheek, a single tear trickled, leaving a hot saline trail that burned against the cold air.

"His neck," she whispered in English, forcing her eyes to hold Mikhail's gaze.

He nodded. "We will help him."

She shook her head, not daring to believe he was a friend. If she was wrong…

A thought came to mind and she gasped. "What color are his eyes?" she asked. Her plan wasn't foolproof, but it was better than nothing.

Mikhail cocked his head to the side. "Blue."

Kate scoffed, her gaze narrowing. They were hardly any old blue.

"Bright, like a sapphire," he continued.

Kate sucked in a breath to respond, but before she

could, a hand clamped over her mouth. Another grabbed her wrist. Her finger squeezed and a single gunshot rang out into the night.

"Get him!" a male voice ordered as she was dragged backward. Commotion erupted around her. Growling. Cursing. Barked commands and replies.

Her own muffled screams added to the fray. "No! No! Don't hurt him!" Fighting the hold that wrapped around her, she kicked and flailed and squirmed to get free.

"Clear!" someone called. "Oh, shit, Mikhail. It's bad."

Kate's body screamed at the separation from her vampire. The palm of her hand burst into pins and needles. Her throat went tight and dry. She had to get to him.

He was hers. *Hers!*

"Damnit, Leo! Get control of her. I hear sirens," a voice demanded.

"Stop fighting," came a gruff voice at her ear. "Damn it. Be still, human."

She slammed to the ground and the weight of a knee fell on her chest. Big hands pinned her arms to her sides. Barely able to breathe and her eyesight blurred from the blow to her head, Kate went limp.

A harsh masculine face appeared right before her, his gray eyes—*good-guy eyes*—boring into hers. "Calm. Sleep. Now," he intoned.

Her mind went foggy. Darkness closed in around her.

Deep sorrow surrounded her. She'd lost him. That old feeling of foreboding and looming tragedy returned. Now she knew why she'd been feeling that way.

She'd had a purpose. Find her vampire. Protect him. Save him. But she'd failed.

And that devastating thought was the last thing she knew.

Nikolai floated on the edge of consciousness, not wanting to wake from the dream. In it, he was no longer alone, but had a mate who walked at his side. He didn't know what she looked like, but the sound of her voice, the smell of her skin, the taste of her blood.

Those he would never forget.

Sated by the sacred crimson nectar that flowed from her veins, Nikolai covered her body with his. Entered her. Howled his masculine satisfaction. Moving in her was a revelation of ecstasy and belonging. She clutched at his shoulders and murmured in his ear, *You're gonna be all right. You're gonna be all right.*

His angel, always taking care of him.

"My lord? Wake up. You are safe," came a deep, familiar voice.

He didn't want to leave her, to leave that place where he wasn't alone.

"Come on, brother. Wake up."

Nikolai surfaced as if he'd been trapped under water for days. Brain sluggish, eyes bleary, mouth full of cotton. He gasped and choked as he tried to make use of his thick tongue.

"Nikolai?" Mikhail's voice sounded as if from a distance.

In the dim light of the room, Nikolai struggled to make sense of the shapes around him. Slowly, *too damn slowly*, his eyes regained the ability to focus.

Elbows braced on his knees, Mikhail sat in a chair by the side of his bed. Or, *a* bed, anyway. White walls and blankets. This wasn't his room. An infirmary, then, and not the one in their city headquarters. They'd brought him to Vasilievskoe, his ancestral estate about an hour outside Moscow.

In that moment, as their gazes met, his friend's brown eyes looked as ancient as he actually was. His head sagged on his shoulders and he clasped his hands where they hung between his knees. "I want to fucking kill you."

Nikolai chuffed out a breath. "Mishka," he said, infusing an apology into his friend's nickname.

"Don't Mishka me."

He deserved the other man's anger. What could he say? "I'm sorry."

Mikhail cursed and shoved out of his seat, the chair screeching against the tile floor. He paced and muttered under his breath. The other man still wore his fighting gear, twisting Nikolai's gut with guilt.

"How long have I been out?" Nikolai managed to ask as he heaved himself into a sitting position with a groan. The movement made him aware that IVs were attached to the crooks of both arms. And, damn, but everything hurt.

"It's early afternoon. About ten hours." Mikhail whirled on him. "Ten goddamn hours I didn't know if my king, my friend, my brother, would die or live to see another night."

He winced at the volume of his friend's outrage. "I was stupid."

"You were fucking moronic." He braced his hands on his hips and glared.

The situation wasn't funny, not in the least, but Nikolai felt the corners of his lips rise. "I'll concede the point." Few others had the balls to talk to him this way, but he and Mikhail had always been close, almost like true-blooded brothers. His stomach plummeted. Kyril and Evgeny were gone, but Mikhail was here, and Nikolai was going out of his way to piss on his friendship, wasn't he.

"Look, Mishka—"

"Save it. I know, all right? I loved them, too. I lost them, too. They might not have been blooded brothers, but they were still my brothers. Like you. Since we were young. So I get it. I do. But I swear to Christ—" He covered his mouth and turned away.

Nikolai cleared the lump from his throat, cursing himself for failing Mikhail exactly as he knew he would, and dragged them back to safer ground. "So, give me the rundown on my condition."

Mikhail turned and crossed his arms. "Broken femur and scapula. Bullet passed through the former, lodged in the latter. Doc got it out on the table. Hit to the right side of your neck took out your jugular and nicked your carotid. Lost half your volume of blood. He patched you up, though, and set up the transfusion before we brought you here. Says you'll survive to be a pain in the ass another day."

Ignoring the gibe, Nikolai frowned. How the hell had he survived such injuries?

No doubt about it, Anton was a master surgeon, but the blood loss alone…not to mention the poison…

A deep sense of something like déjà vu came over Nikolai. He frowned, suddenly certain he'd forgotten something important. He scrubbed a hand through his hair, hampered some by the connected tubes. "Jesus. What a mess."

Mikhail sighed. "Yeah. Understatement of the century,

my friend. Even more complicated by the girl. We need to decide what to do with her. She's seen a lot."

Nikolai narrowed his gaze and tried to decipher the words, but he had no idea what Mikhail was talking about. "What girl?"

Staring at him, Mikhail dropped back into the chair beside the bed. "What girl? The one who saved your life."

CHAPTER 5

VWK

Kate woke up disoriented, hurting, and pissed off.
She eased into a sitting position, the back of her head throbbing harder as she rose, and tried to make sense of her dim surroundings.

Small, spartan cot, an empty wooden table with a single chair. She looked to the right and gasped. Bars. An iron-barred door.

Was she in jail? Or—she peered at the rough, stone walls—a freaking dungeon?

She flew to her feet and moaned. The small room spun around her. With her head in her hands, she sucked deep breaths until the dizziness passed. Clenching her eyelids, she prayed she'd been having a nightmare. She opened her eyes.

Oh, shit. No such luck.

Outrage bubbled up from Kate's gut. Surveying the room, she located a high-tech security camera in one corner. Old-looking cell paired with modern surveillance equipment.

The vampires had her. Had to be.

Kate glared into the camera. "Let me out of here, damn you. Do you hear me? You have no right." Her voice rose with each word until she was shouting, the sound echoing off the stone. Trying the door next, she shouted, "Let me out of here!"

Holding a bar to steady herself, she looked down at her body. Coat gone. Mace gone. Cell phone gone. Her hand flew to her lower back. Gun gone.

But her clothes…they were the same. And they were covered in blood. Her jeans were red and stiff from hips to knees. Smears of blood ruined her pale blue sweater, and the sleeve of it was shredded. She sucked in a breath. Gauze circled her forearm from the heel of her thumb to nearly the crook of her elbow. Spots of maroon seeped through the layers.

The details of the night flooded back to her in vivid color.

Her vampire.

His attack.

Her acceptance.

The arrival of the others.

Kate slid down to her butt, wincing as her tailbone eased against the stone floor, and sagged against the bars. Eyes stinging and throat tight, a confusing maelstrom of emotions washed over her like rough waves in a storm, swamping, tumbling, turning her round and round.

Fear and bewilderment released her tears onto her cheeks. A vampire had fed from her. And she'd let him. She hadn't fought, not really.

Worse. In the end, she'd liked it, craved it, wanted to give him everything he needed. She'd wanted more.

How could she have so easily turned her back on everything she'd believed? Sitting there on the dirty floor of a freaking dungeon, Kate didn't even know who she'd been in those long minutes in that alley.

Rage also flowed through her and tensed every muscle in her body until she trembled. *She'd* found him. *She'd* helped him. *She'd* saved him. He was *hers*. And *they'd* taken him away, ripped him from her arms, literally.

And now she didn't even know if he'd survived.

The emotions completely contradicted each other, but that didn't make them any less true, any less real.

And if that wasn't enough, Kate's mind struggled with another set of feelings she would rather just pretend didn't exist.

Desire. Hot and torturous.

His scent clung to her, concentrated as it was on her clothes, her skin. It made her…want. What? Everything. She thirsted. She hungered. She felt an urgent emptiness between her legs like nothing she'd ever before experienced.

What was happening to her?

Heaving a deep breath, Kate shook her head. No. Enough. She fisted the wetness off her face and wiped the useless tears on her sweater. *Shit*. If only her head didn't hurt so bad she could think more clearly.

In the distance, a door clinked as if a lock was disengaged. Footsteps echoed against the stonework.

Using the bars, Kate pulled herself up and stepped back from the door.

A vampire in all black appeared on the other side. Tall, lean, dark blond hair to his shoulders. The left side bore a braid—the mark of a warrior. His features were no less attractive for how unfriendly they were. He had familiar gray eyes.

They stared at each other until the warrior finally threaded his hand through the bars and held out a bottle of water.

Kate crossed her arms. "Like I'd trust that."

"If we wanted to kill you, you'd be dead already. Besides, the cap is sealed." He thrust the bottle closer. His voice confirmed he was the same one who had hypnotized her in the parking lot, except it was gentler now. He shrugged and placed the bottle on the floor inside the bars. "Suit yourself." His gaze looked her over from head to toe, and then he turned.

"Wait," she said. "The vampire…where is he? How is he?" The questions were out of her mouth before she'd even thought to ask them. But then, she burned to know.

The man's expression darkened, his eyes narrowed. This look she remembered from earlier. "He is of no concern to you."

Kate scoffed and stifled the more confrontational response on the tip of her tongue. "Like hell. I saved him." She held out her arm. "And I've got this nice little memento to prove it." Actually, she had no idea what the wound looked like, but it stung and ached like crazy.

He grunted. "That doesn't make you special. That makes you convenient."

His words struck her like a punch to the gut. Wasn't that the very thing she most feared as she'd once considered the possibility of a future with vampires? Dizziness returned and made her eyes throb, but Kate held her stance. No way she was letting him see how much pain she was in, how much his words had affected her. "When can I go?" she asked, voice softer than before.

The vampire shifted feet. "I don't have that information. I just have water. Drink it or don't."

Glaring, Kate threw out her hands. "What is your problem? What did I ever do to you?"

His gaze narrowed and dark light seemed to flare behind his eyes. He stared as if debating, then shook his head. "Drink the water. You lost a lot of blood."

Cursing under her breath, Kate watched his retreating form through the bars, totally bewildered by the exchange.

Nikolai stared at Mikhail, his brain churning on the words *The one who saved your life*.

His dream came back to him, only…it wasn't a dream. Was it? Not all of it, anyway.

Ignoring the hit-by-a-bus pain that racked his body, Nikolai flew forward and swung his legs off the bed. He ripped the IV from his right arm and reached for the left.

"My lord!" Mikhail grabbed his wrist, stilling him. "What are you doing?"

Nikolai ignored his friend's use of the title. Despite refusing to lead his kingdom, he couldn't get his warriors to treat him as if they were all the same. And they *were*. Hell, the others were arguably better—they hadn't dishonored themselves, and across the board had handled losing two of their comrades far better. After a while, he'd mostly stopped making an issue of the "my lord" crap.

He shrugged off Mikhail's grip and glared up at him. "Take me to her."

The warrior shook his head. "You're hours out of surgery, still low on blood volume, and now bleeding again." He sighed and gestured at the crook of Nikolai's arm. "She can wait."

His tone regarding the girl rankled Nikolai. "She saved me," he said, mostly to himself, trying out the idea. He struggled to wade through the pain and disorientation to remember what had actually happened. He could hear her voice, feel her arms embracing him… "No… Fuck, no. I attacked her." He nailed Mikhail with a stare. "Didn't I?"

"I don't know." He scrubbed his face. "When we got there, she was holding you. Defending you with your own gun. Her wrist was a mess, though."

Nikolai tore out the second IV and rose to his feet before Mikhail had a chance to react. She'd not only saved him, but held him, protected him. He had to see her. To put a face to the deeds, to the jumble of emotions roiling within. "Get me some clothes."

"Nikolai—"

"Clothes, damnit." Mikhail nodded and left, and Nikolai sagged against the mattress.

Why the hell was he acting this way? So she'd fed him. So what? Feeding from humans wasn't remarkable, though none had ever rearranged his insides the way the mere idea of this one seemed to.

He just needed to put a face to the actions. Appease his curiosity. That would drive away this incessant yearning to get to her, to be with her.

He pushed off the bed and crossed to the sink. Aw, he looked like hell.

Blood-matted, tangled hair. He peeled back the thick gauze on the right side of his neck. The crisscrossing black of the stitches stood out in sharp relief against the angry red of the healing wound. A few more hours and he could remove them altogether. He dropped the bandage to the trash can.

The cold water he splashed on his face made him yearn for a shower. Well, since Mikhail was taking his sweet-ass time…

A small bathroom in the corner had a shower stall his body filled completely. But it did the job. The water ran red around his feet—leftover blood, nothing fresh. His lineage was strong, virile, granting him the ability to heal quickly.

And the girl's blood out in the field, when things had been do-or-die critical, didn't hurt, either. In fact, it had been the difference between life and death.

He whipped a towel off the rack and scrubbed it over his hair and skin, wincing as he passed over his neck. He wrapped a second towel around his hips. When he walked back into the infirmary room, he found Mikhail sitting in the chair waiting. He jutted his chin toward the bed, directing Nikolai's gaze to a pile of clothing with a manila folder sitting on top. He picked it up. "What's this?"

"Information. On the girl. She had a passport and cell phone. Leo ran them."

Nikolai flipped the folder open.

Katherine Ann Bordessa. From Washington, D.C. American exchange student at the Moscow University for the Humanities. Fluent in English, Russian, and French.

He scanned farther down. "Oh, goddammit."

"Yeah," Mikhail said as he rose from his seat.

"Her parents sit on the North American Electorate Council." His desire to speak to her went from curiosity to necessity. He needed to learn what happened between them and ensure it didn't escalate into some sort of diplomatic incident. For now, he knew enough. He chucked the papers to the bed and grabbed some clothes.

"Will there be anything else, my lord?"

"Stop calling me that?"

Mikhail just stared at him, mouth shut but posture speaking volumes.

Nikolai stepped into black pants, part of his typical street-fighting uniform, and yanked them to his waist. He reached for the little leather pouch he always carried on him. That his friend thought to bring this to him made his throat go tight. He cleared it as he tucked the memento in his front pocket.

"Where is she?" he asked, tugging a T-shirt over his head. When Mikhail didn't answer, he turned.

The warrior's expression had him bracing for bad news. The man pursed his lips, then said, "The dungeon, rear cell."

CHAPTER 6

VWK

A series of metal clinks preceded the pounding of boots down the corridor outside Kate's cell. Weighed down by exhaustion, hunger, an oppressive headache, and a sore butt, she stayed seated on the cot, back against the wall, knees drawn up in front of her.

A low, terse exchange echoed off the stonework a moment before two big bodies filled the doorway in front of her.

My vampire!

The possessive reaction was instinctual. Even though of course he wasn't hers. And she didn't want him to be. Right? That was why she was in Moscow in the first place…

She flew forward on the bed, her feet settling on the floor. She fought a groan and gripped the metal edge of the frame to keep her balance. *This damn headache.* But it didn't matter, because her vampire was standing before her.

Conscious. Healthy. More gorgeous than any man she had ever seen.

Those eyes. Those bright sapphire eyes. That's what she

noticed first—not just their incredible color, but their haunted intensity, the way she could almost feel them raking over her in return. Brown hair with golden highlights flowed to just past his broad shoulders, though it wasn't braided like that of the black-haired warrior who stood at his side.

She sucked in a breath and glared at the other man. *He* was the one who had pretended to want to talk, but had really just distracted her so the gray-eyed vampire could jump her.

Her vampire cut his gaze back and forth between them. He bit out a question Kate couldn't understand because he asked it in German. She frowned. They knew she spoke Russian, so what were they saying that they didn't want her to know?

The exchange went on for a moment, and Kate pushed off the bed and took a step toward the door. Another. She just needed to make sure he was really okay. After everything. And the closer she walked, the farther her body wanted her to keep going.

Both vampires turned to look at her and she froze.

Heart kicking up in her chest, she met her vampire's bright eyes and asked, "Are you okay?"

Light seemed to flicker behind his gaze, which dragged down her body and focused for a long moment on her blood-covered legs. He cocked his head as if not understanding her, though she knew she'd spoken in flawless Russian.

Finally, he met her eyes and nodded. "I am well. And I understand you had something to do with that."

Kate's stomach flip-flopped at the sound of his voice, deep and much more commanding than what she'd heard in her mind. She felt it like a physical touch. She shrugged. "I tried."

"Katherine—" the other one interjected "we are in a bit—"

She groaned at his use of her name. She'd never made introductions—she'd never been given the chance. "My passport. Right? You took my passport?"

The man nodded. "It was necessary. Your belongings will be returned to you."

Kate crossed her arms, not sure whether to trust his words or assume they were simply a ruse, same as he had done in the alley when he'd distracted her. Which was where she'd heard his name. "And you're Mikhail. Is that right? Since you know so much about me, it's only fair I know a little about you in return." Her gaze shifted from the dark vampire to the one she'd saved, who wore an expression that appeared almost amused.

"Yes, I'm Mikhail—"

"Nikolai," her vampire blurted. "I'm Nikolai, Katherine."

A thrill shot down her spine. She loved the sound of her name on his voice, as if his tongue caressed the letters. "Yes. I go by Kate, though."

He shook his head. "Katherine is a beautiful name."

"My lord—"

Nikolai held up a hand. The gesture was full of an authority the other vampire responded to immediately.

My lord? What was that about?

The brown-haired vampire scowled. "Leave us, Mikhail. And give me the keys."

Intrigued, she watched the warrior obey and depart with a final glance her way.

Alone again, Kate wasn't sure what to say. God, he was tall and broad. She remembered the muscular feel of those shoulders. She wanted to run her hands over him and prove to herself he was well. She wanted to press her face into his neck. Instead, she stood there watching, waiting, hating the iron bars that separated them.

But maybe it was better to have the barrier. It would keep her from caving into his allure as easily as she'd done before.

What she couldn't tolerate anymore was the awkward silence. "I was worried about you. I'm glad you're better." That odd tingling returned to her palm and Kate fisted her fingers without thinking about it. The movement pulled at the wound on her arm. She winced.

Standing firm and still on the far side of the door, he said, "Your concern…" He shook his head. "Thank you." His gaze dropped to the movement of her hand. "I am better, but it appears you are worse for our meeting."

Heat bloomed on Kate's cheeks. She wrapped her arm behind her back. "Oh, well…" A dozen responses vied for airtime, but that's all she could manage. The deep reverence of his words and his raw masculine beauty, all rough edges and hard angles, stole her breath.

And she was so conflicted about the feeding she could hardly think straight. How could she both cherish and regret the memory of it? She ducked her head.

He released a breath and recaptured her attention. "I have to ask you, Katherine, how did you come to find me?" His voice was low and deep, his intense gaze studying her.

Maybe she imagined it, but he seemed fixated on the bloodied parts of her clothing. She shifted feet, self-consciousness making her want to squirm. She tucked her hair behind her ear. "It was a complete coincidence. I was walking to the metro—"

"In the middle of the night?"

She frowned at the harder edge to his tone. Was this some kind of interrogation? The thought squeezed her heart. After everything she'd done, he didn't trust her? And why was it she cared? "I couldn't sleep. I thought a walk would help."

"The university is twenty kilometers away from the city."

"Which is why I was taking the metro." She sighed. So tired. "Why all these questions?"

"We need to understand what happened tonight."

His distance and dispassionate tone left her feeling empty and bereft. And so stupid. As if anything unique had happened between them. As if he would think she deserved any special consideration.

"Well, here's what you need to know: I found you unconscious and bleeding, tried to help you, got bit for my trouble—" she pulled her arm from behind her back and thrust it toward him "—and then got tackled, kidnapped, and dumped in a dungeon. Does that help?"

The volume of her accusations hurt her own head. On top of the pain and the blood loss and the adrenaline let-down, it was more than she could take. She swayed, hating that she was showing weakness in front of him, but unable to hold herself together any longer.

Nikolai was completely enthralled by the woman standing before him.

Beautiful in her assertiveness. Bravery proven over and again. Wearing so much of his blood he went hard between his legs. She appealed to his body, intrigued his mind. His right hand tingled and twitched. He fisted against the foreign sensation.

Katherine went unsteady on her feet even as her angry words still echoed against the stone walls. Her uncharacteristic display of weakness put him into motion.

He unlocked and opened the door as she turned for the cot, and wrapped a steadying arm around her shoulders before her knees buckled. Nikolai sucked in a breath at the warm feel of her in his arms, at the soft brush of her hair against his hand, at the feminine scent of her skin, infused as it was with the remnants of his blood.

Her voice, her touch, her scent—all these he remembered. Now having seen her beautiful face—the long chocolate waves and ice-blue eyes were a killer combination—his memories of the night became clearer and crisper in his mind. He was mesmerized, fascinated.

And she was…she was shaking.

"Sit," he said, guiding her down and resisting the urge to press her back against the bed, to feel her under him. Instead, he crouched at her knees.

"I'm fine. Just a headache."

Nikolai frowned and shouted for Leo, knowing he was manning the security booth and would hear him on the camera's audio feed. Katherine jumped and cringed at the sound of his voice. He grimaced. "Damn, I'm sorry."

She shrugged and licked her lips, those pale blue eyes not quite meeting his. "Just a bump on the head. I'm fine."

There was something she wasn't saying. He sucked in a breath and was about to ask, when he heard a voice from behind .

"My lord," Leo said.

Katherine's eyebrows flew up at the appellation. She narrowed her gaze as if questioning him. "She needs pain medicine. Yes?" He tilted his head and scanned her face. High cheekbones, full mouth, creamy pale skin. Too pale.

"Yes, please."

"And food, I suspect." It was more than a suspicion, he could feel the hunger rolling off of her. This connection to her needs and emotions was unexpected, and unwelcome. Still, he owed her. "When did you last eat?"

Her eyes flicked over his shoulder, then back to him. "I'm not sure. What time is it?"

"Pushing three in the afternoon."

She looked down and slid her clasped hands between her thighs. "Dinner, last night."

Nikolai sucked in a breath and whirled on Leo. "Has she not been offered any food?"

Leo's eyebrows flew to his hairline. His mouth dropped open, and his gaze cut to the floor by the door to the cell, where a bottle of water sat untouched.

"She has had nothing at all?"

"I'm sorry, my lord." Leo bowed his head. "I'll get something, uh, now. I'll just—" He thumbed over his shoulder and left.

Nikolai crossed the room and retrieved the bottle, then returned to his crouch before her. He removed the lid and held the water out to her. "Drink it. I know I must've taken more from you than I should've. You are probably severely dehydrated."

Katherine eyed the bottle, swallowing hard enough to be audible. "Why do they all listen to you?"

"Because I'm a pain in the ass if they don't." Saying any more would lead to conversations there wasn't a chance in hell he would have. With her. With anyone. "Now, drink."

She arched an eyebrow at him, and the commentary regarding his command was crystal clear. He almost smiled, except it was obvious she wanted the water, so why didn't she take it?

All at once, he knew.

It was the same concern he would've had in her position. He put the bottle to his lips and took a long sip, then offered it to her again.

Her shoulders sagged and she accepted the bottle, drinking nearly half of it at once. Twin reactions coursed through Nikolai—regret that she didn't trust him enough to take the water before he'd proven it clean, and satisfaction at seeing one of her needs sated.

And at having a hand in that.

Truly, he couldn't blame her for the mistrust. Hadn't he approached her the same way? Wary. Questioning. Not to mention his brethren had thrown her in a dungeon.

The satisfaction, though, that was a whole other animal. In and of itself, something to be distrusted. Because the root of it lay in his fascination with her, desire for her—a desire he needed to ignore.

If the past six months taught him anything, it was that he could never again tolerate such loss. No way he would ever put himself in the position of feeling this kind of pain again. Evgeny's and Kyril's deaths had left a gaping hole in the center of his being.

Shit. Why was he even thinking about any of this?

Katherine rested the nearly empty bottle on her thigh and glanced up at him. A glossy sheen covered her bottom lip. Nikolai's mouth fell open as his respiration increased.

The plump, wet skin called to him, beckoned. To taste it…

All at once, his mind went blank and he could focus on nothing else. Unconsciously, he leaned in, watching as her lips parted and her tongue snaked out to wet her top lip, too. Their eyes met. Hers were hooded and intense, heaven in a stare. He held her gaze as he moved closer. Her scent added to her allure, surrounding and confusing him. The smell of his own blood, on her, followed fast behind, building within his chest a deep, hot feeling of male satisfaction. Christ, he loved her wearing his blood. Were it on her skin, he wouldn't be able to stop himself from devouring it. Devouring her. Warm, quick exhalations fell against his lips.

He shouldn't do this, he really fucking shouldn't, but he had to, he had to know—

"My lord, I brought—" Footsteps ended abruptly in the doorway behind him.

Nikolai wrenched back and rose to his feet, his heart hammering against his breastbone. Disappointment warred with relief in his mind. What the hell was he doing? He fixed a glare on Leo and nodded to the table.

Eyes down, the young warrior crossed the room and dropped the tray to show his displeasure.

"Something on your mind, Leo?"

"No, my lord," he said, gaze still averted.

"Didn't think so." Skin prickly, muscles tense, fangs aching, Nikolai was pissed off now and not sure why. "Is Anton here?"

Leo shook his head. "Stayed in the city once you were stabilized."

Nikolai didn't miss the unusual gruffness to the kid's voice. "Call him and tell him to come. She needs to be examined. Let me know the minute he arrives. Now, go." Leo lifted his eyes enough to communicate understanding and gave a single nod.

Feeling edgy and restless, Nikolai watched him leave and then grasped the tray and placed it on the bed.

Wide, leery eyes peered up at him. The sound of her heart was thunderous in his ears. "Examined?"

Nikolai crouched again. "You're hurt. We have a doctor on staff. I would like him to look at you. Will you allow it?"

"Um. I'm just a little banged up." Her gaze dropped to the tray.

Her implicit refusal stoked the fire of his mounting anger. "Christ, Katherine, you're a little more than banged up." Before he'd even thought to do it, he yanked her wrist from her lap and tore the gauze free.

She gasped and pulled back, but his grip on her elbow held her in place.

Holy Mother of God.

He was an animal. A fucking animal.

Chewed. It was the only word to describe what he saw.

From wrist to mid-forearm, her arm was a landscape of red and purple. One, two, three times his fangs had penetrated her flesh—and not cleanly, and at least twice had his other teeth broken her skin, too. Angry bruises in the form of fingers—his fingers—circled her arm in several places.

"Stop. You're hurting me."

Her words slapped him.

He released her, suddenly aware of how hard he'd been gripping her elbow and hand. She cradled her arm against her stomach, remnants of gauze still clinging, and hid the worst of the injuries from his gaze. But the image was seared onto his brain.

His throat went raw, as if he'd swallowed glass.

His head sagging on his shoulders, he raked his hands through his hair. He couldn't stop hurting others, could he? And to hurt *her*, of all people. Maybe they'd all just be better off if he—

"Hey," she said softly. The light touch of her hand landed on the back of his head. After a moment, she stroked him. Slow. Gentle.

Out of nowhere, a hazy memory slammed into his brain. The soft drags of her fingers in his hair, when he'd been injured, when she'd given him permission to feed from her vein. How shaken she must've been, how much pain he'd clearly inflicted, and yet she'd shown him tenderness, compassion.

"I'll see the doctor, okay? You know, as long as he's a real doctor, and all." The soft cup of her hand petted over his hair again.

For a long moment, Nikolai absorbed the incredible warmth and gentleness of her touch. It had been so long since he'd allowed himself the smallest pleasure. He didn't deserve it, but that didn't keep him from wanting it, from needing it, like air.

Like blood.

Resigned to see fear or hatred or disgust in her eyes, Nikolai lifted his head.

She smiled at him, her eyes filled with what looked like understanding and concern. "Okay?"

Nikolai's chest flooded with a foreign warm pressure. The hand that he rubbed against his sternum ached and the meaning of that sensation niggled at his consciousness.

What was she doing to him?

He swallowed, hard, and nodded, the flash fire of his rage dying as quickly as it had roared to life. "Okay."

CHAPTER 7

Feeling that odd pull to her again, exacerbated by a deep and growing need to heal her, to care for her, to make her better, Nikolai turned his attention to the tray. Next to the plate of grilled shashlik was a pill bottle. He handed it to her. "Will this work for you?"

She read the label and nodded, then set about removing the plastic safety wrapping securing the cap. Her cheeks pinked, intensifying her luscious scent and making Nikolai realize he was watching her every move. He sat back on his ass, knees drawn up in front of him, and put a little distance between them as she swallowed the pills.

Eyeing the tray, she licked her lips. "Do you, uh, do you want some? Or, oh, maybe you don't eat…"

"I do, but it's for you." Nikolai's mouth went dry at the offer. After everything she'd given him, she was willing to offer more?

"I can share."

"Please."

Shrugging, Katherine picked up a shashlik skewer and pulled a piece of marinated, grilled beef from one end.

"I hope this is to your liking. The only human foods we eat are meat and spirits, and I'm sure the staff didn't have time to prepare for our arrival."

"It smells great. Anyway, I'm so hungry anything would taste good, so…" She ate the beef from her fingers, and sucked the juice from her thumb.

Her teeth, sinking into the rare flesh. The pink juice on her lips. The little, throaty sounds of pleasure and satiation. Nikolai's erection turned to steel. Each bite taunted and seduced him. It was everything he could do to sit still and let her finish her meal.

Maybe diverting his attention from her mouth would help. His gaze dropped to the shapely fit of her sweater over the round fullness of her breasts. His palms ached to feel the heavy warmth of them, his fangs throbbed at the thought of penetrating the perfect mounds with his bite while his cock filled the cleft between her thighs.

He heaved a breath and forced his eyes to keep moving, but there was no place safe to look. The blood—his blood—smeared across the hem of her sweater and coating the front of her jeans from waist to knees unleashed a deep yearning in his gut.

He *wanted* her to have his blood, but not accidentally. He wanted her to have it because he'd knowingly offered and she'd willingly, wantonly accepted.

He sucked in a breath. There was only one way that happened. If they were mates.

Which was something he could never have. Not after

what he'd done. He didn't deserve the comfort, the solace, the satisfaction that a mate could bring to his life.

But, Jesus, she was making him think, making him consider, making him want.

No.

"How old are you?" he asked.

She swallowed the bite she was chewing and wiped her mouth with a napkin. "Twenty."

Nikolai dropped his head to his knees with a groan.

"Almost twenty-one," she said, cracking open a new bottle of water Leo had brought in with the tray.

His gaze cut back to her. "When?"

She wiped her wet lips with the back of her hand. "My birthday's on Friday."

What kind of fate would lead him to this brave, beautiful creature, a woman who had saved and protected him, at the height of her blood power for just four more days, when he could never claim her, never have her? Not for keeps.

She rose from the bed and stepped around him to return the tray to the table.

Her scent wrapped around his heart, his cock. Heat flickered across his right palm. "Goddammit," he snapped.

Because all the signs were there.

"What?" she said.

He couldn't let himself be seduced by an impossible idea. He sprung to his feet and made for the door, still open from his earlier rushed entry. "I have to go."

"Why?" She followed after him, the alluring beat of her heart and intoxicating femininity revealing her place within the room.

He couldn't stop, couldn't reply, couldn't look at her. If he did, there'd be no going back. He grasped the edge of the door.

Small hands fisted in the back of his shirt. "Wait. Why are you leaving? I mean, did I—"

He halted, heart slamming against his sternum, fangs stretched out and aching. "Release me," he rasped.

She heaved a shaky breath he felt against his arm. "I… can't."

"Release. Me," he said louder. Competing emotions warred within him until he thought he might split apart.

"Nikolai—"

It was his name rolling off her tongue that did it.

He whirled and buried his hands in her hair. He pulled her to him, causing them both to stumble, and then he turned her and backed her into the ancient bars of the door. It clicked shut, sealing them in and cutting off the last of his restraint.

Tilting her head back, Nikolai devoured her mouth. His lips sucked, his tongue explored, his fangs rubbed against her moist flesh. *Oh, God*, she was so sweet and warm and wet. He stepped into her, forcing their bodies together from chest to thighs. And, goddammit, she was soft everywhere he was hard.

Her hands curled around his neck and climbed into his hair, fingers tangling and tugging. She pulled him in tighter and surrendered to the kiss. She met him stroke for stroke, their tongues curling and twining together. Her tongue stroking at his fangs until he was sure he would lose his fucking mind.

Until Nikolai no longer knew who was surrendering to whom.

※

Kate was adrift in sensation. She felt engulfed by the heat rolling off Nikolai's big body, which was hunched around her possessively. His hard muscles flexed and bunched against her, setting her on fire everywhere they touched. His warm, spicy smell invaded her brain until it was the only thing she knew. His tongue in her mouth, his hands all over her—she couldn't fight it.

In truth, she didn't want to.

Earlier, when it seemed like he'd planned to kiss her, she'd resisted the idea, kept her body from succumbing to the instinctual pull to lean toward his. But now, even though he represented everything she'd never wanted, she could no longer deny that something about him spoke to her body, her psyche, her very soul.

Kate was totally and completely seduced by her vampire.

Her vampire.

A groan sounded from deep in his throat, conveying pure, desperate need, and he pressed harder into her. Against her back, the iron bars formed an inescapable cage. In front of her, his body towered over and confined her, emphasizing the thick ridge of his erection straining against her belly.

She'd never felt more free than she did in that moment, utterly trapped by Nikolai.

And if his preternatural power wasn't prominent enough

in the sheer strength of his body around hers, the hard edges of his fangs against her lips and tongue wouldn't let her forget it. Fascinated despite herself, she wrapped her tongue around a fang and flicked at it. Nikolai growled and ground the steel length of his cock into her hip.

Kate went hot and wet between her legs, completely overwhelmed by her body's ecstatic reaction to his. Never had she imagined she'd be capable of such euphoria. She'd certainly never felt it before.

Maybe she wouldn't again.

The thought unleashed a current of panic into the lust flowing through her, because what she was feeling for Nikolai was so much more than physical.

Her heart tripped over the pain he seemed to carry in the cast of his eyes and the set of his shoulders. He unleashed every protective and nurturing instinct in her body—*she* wanted to be the one to take away whatever hurt him, or to comfort him, at the very least. And there was absolutely no denying that all the angst and restlessness that had been making her feel unsettled in her own skin lately, that had been getting worse and worse these past weeks, mostly disappeared in his presence.

The question was…why?

A little voice inside her told her she *knew* why, but but this his big hand fisted in her hair and tilted her head further back, opening her further to the urgent demand of his kisses.

There was no refuting the physical attraction between them, that was for damn sure. As close as they were, it was miles too far apart. Kate embraced his big shoulders, pulling, tugging, needing him closer. Her body remembered her unfulfilled need from the night before, spiking her arousal and creating an urgent ache between her legs.

God, she wanted him…wanted him…in her.

Her hands fell to his waist and gripped at the fabric of his tee, burrowing under. His skin was warm and smooth over hard, flexing muscles. She pushed the shirt higher, needing to feel more, explore more, to know if he was this amazing everywhere.

Abruptly, Nikolai wrenched back from the kiss, and he looked every bit of the creature he was. Lips red, mouth open, fangs protruding, eyes aglow. Unease flared in her stomach.

He was going to pull away. Like before.

She dug her nails into his sides, willing him to stay. He stared at her for a long moment, then finally reached back with one arm and tore the shirt over his head.

Relief crashed through her and she moaned in admiration of the artwork decorating his skin. A massive stylized black eagle spread its wings across his pecs and its tail curled down over the carved muscles of his stomach. Its golden claws wielded swords, and its regal head bore a crown. It was a fascinating, beautiful play on the Russian coat of arms. Symbols she didn't recognize adorned his right arm, from wrist to biceps, the black ink against his fair skin such a stunning, attractive contrast.

Inexperience be damned, she was drawn to taste him. Pushing onto tiptoes, Kate pressed an openmouthed kiss over his nipple and sucked him in. Oh, he tasted of that incredible spice he wore on his skin. She couldn't get enough. She kissed and licked across his chest, and his hands fisted in her hair—holding her close or tugging her away, she couldn't be sure.

He grasped her chin and nudged her mouth up, then kissed her eyes, her nose, the corner of her lips. "So beautiful."

Each kiss, each touch, each word washed away the last of her uncertainty until she knew she would give him anything he wanted. That didn't mean she wasn't scared, because she was, but everything in her, down to the very marrow of her bones, told her he was worth the risk.

"May I...I want to do something for you," he said around a kiss.

"Anything," she whispered, her lips trailing down the hard angle of his jaw to his neck. Tight crisscrosses of black thread were the only evidence of his terrible wound. Taking care to be gentle, she pressed a featherlight kiss atop his stitches.

"Oh, angel," he groaned. The sound rumbled against her breasts, adding to the electric tingling making her pussy slick and needy. He grasped the hem of her sweater, then his whole face slid into a scowl. "Goddammit." Looking over his shoulder, he barked. "Camera off. Now."

As she watched, the red blinking light on the unit went dark.

Her sweater was up and over her head as the heat of a blush warmed her face, but she was so deep into Nikolai, she found she couldn't think long on her embarrassment that someone—some *vampire*—had been watching them together. She gasped at the sensation of the cold bars pressing stripes into the skin of her back. Big hands cupped the sides of her breasts and his mouth fell to her cleavage. He kissed and nibbled, dragging the tips of his fangs across the mounds in a tantalizing threat. She threw her head back against the door and silently begged him to do it.

Just do it.

Oh, shit, she was so far down the rabbit hole with him. And, God help her, she wouldn't have it any other way.

She carded her fingers into his hair, loving the thick silkiness of it, and embraced him as he sucked her nipple through the thin satin of her bra.

He gripped the back of her left wrist and pulled it to his mouth. "This is what I must…" He trailed off and laved his tongue against the red marks on her arm.

She moaned as his saliva tingled against the cuts and abrasions. It didn't hurt. Just the opposite. It brought such maddeningly beautiful relief. The sensation ricocheted through her and had her writhing against him. He hummed something that sounded like satisfied approval and slid a thick muscled thigh tight between her legs. She cried out at the glorious friction and couldn't help but rock her hips against him.

He cut his gaze to hers as he licked her forearm with his healing saliva. His eyes were a blazing blue. She could fall into those eyes and be so happy there…

The thought brought another with it, and suspicion sent her heart slamming against her breastbone: *he* was the cause of her angst. Somehow, needing to find Nikolai, protect him, be *with* him was the source of the restlessness and confusion plaguing her all these long months. She'd left the service of the Proffered, and soul deep her body had known that decision put her on the wrong path.

Or maybe it was the right one. Because he was why

she'd come to Moscow. He was why she'd been on that street at that time. Nikolai was the answer to every *why* question she'd ever had.

Given how short she'd known him, her certainty didn't make any sense, but there it was anyway.

The truth of her revelation spiraled through her body and settled itself in every cell. Combined with his tongue, his thigh, his eyes, those little sounds of masculine appreciation—it was all too much. "Oh, God, Nikolai. You have to…" She shook her head, unable to control her breathing, or her body. "You have to stop, or I—"

"Not yet." He pulled his leg away.

She whimpered and flexed off the bars.

The corner of his mouth curled up as he healed her with one last long, languid stroke of his tongue.

"No, no. I have to. Please." She squirmed and ground her belly against his cock. Despite her general inexperience, her body acted on its own instinct, seemingly knowing what, or whom, would bring her the relief and release she nearly screamed for.

"You have to what, angel?"

She hesitated for a few short, quick heartbeats. "I have to…" The word on the tip of her tongue, she clenched her thighs together, burning for the friction he'd given to her moments before. "Oh, God."

"You have to come, yes?" he whispered against her ear. Kate nodded, her stomach flip-flopping at his tone, full of sin and satisfaction. One hand fell to her jeans, tugged at the zipper, ripped the denim open. "I want to wear you on my skin," he said.

Gently but firmly, he slid his fingers under the band of her panties.

The rough pads of his fingertips slid into the soft hair at the top of her mound, and Kate moaned and grabbed the closest bar with her free hand to keep from falling. He kicked at the inside of her shoe. "Open."

Pressed against the iron bars of her dungeon cell, Kate spread her legs. Nikolai's fingers dipped into the slick folds of her pussy, rubbing, flicking, pressing tight circles that stole her breath. He lingered a kiss to the healed skin over her radial artery, then dropped her arm and brought his mouth back to hers. The movement of his lips was slow, reverent, just the beginning of something she knew she'd never forget.

She grabbed a bar with her newly healed hand and just let herself feel the incredible ecstasy he drew from her body.

Forehead resting against hers, he pushed one finger inside her and met her gaze. She gasped, his finger so much bigger than her own, which until this moment had been the sum total of her experience.

"Come on me, Katya. I want to feel it. I want to see it."

"Nikolai," she whimpered, holding his gaze. His finger simultaneously eased the ache and escalated it as he penetrated and thrust, his palm providing more of that glorious friction against her clit. Panting, she couldn't keep from moving her hips and urging more. Inside, her body tightened around his finger.

"Mmm, yes." Licking his lips and drilling his intense, flaring gaze into her eyes, he added a second finger. "Take more of me."

Kate moaned at the fullness, reveled in it, wanted even more—even if her desire scared her. The thought was fleeting. His fingers moved in and out of her in a shallow quick pattern that rocketed all her energy downward, then detonated in a brilliant explosion of light and heat that sent her flying, falling, floating outside herself.

Hanging on the bars, her whole body sagged against him, her weight falling onto his hand between her legs and his chest. She was dimly aware of the approving growl rumbling from deep in his throat.

He wrapped an arm around her back and tugged her hair, gently pulling her head back so he could claim her mouth. The kiss was slow and sensual, full of the promise of more to come. And despite the fact that the room spun around her and she couldn't control the pace or volume of her breathing, more was exactly what she wanted.

She couldn't wait to have the chance to bring him the same incredible ecstasy he'd given her.

Nikolai pulled his hand from between her legs, but didn't leave her skin. Still under the stretched fabric of her panties, his big, warm grip slid around to grasp the naked curve of her hip. His fingers were wet where they dug into her ass, but she couldn't feel embarrassed about it, not after he'd shown her the pleasure her body was capable of experiencing.

He broke the kiss with a gleam in his eye. A cocky smile played around the corners of his mouth. As infuriatingly smug as it was, he wore the good humor so well she could only find it sexy.

"Katya, I —"

An exaggerated cleared throat sounded from just down the stone corridor outside her cell. "My lord, Anton awaits you in the security booth."

Kate sucked in a breath. But neither the voice nor the intrusion of the reality that others probably *knew* what was going on in here were the most alarming thing. Not by far.

Nikolai flew back from her, eyes and head averted as if he'd done something wrong. Breathing hard and scowling, he bent down and retrieved both their shirts. When he stood up, he held her sweater out to her, but didn't look her in the eye.

In almost slow motion, Kate released her hands from the bars, just now realizing Nikolai's actions had frozen her into a spectator as she tried to decipher the marked change in his mood. The moment her hand clutched the soft blue of her sweater, tears pricked the backs of her eyes.

She clutched the cotton to her chest. "Nikolai—"

"Don't," he snapped, his voice low and tight. He yanked his shirt over his head, hiding those beautiful tattoos, hiding himself, from her gaze. "For God's sake, clothe yourself."

Blinking repeatedly to pinch off the threatening tears, Kate slipped back into her sweater. She tugged at the zipper to her jeans, but it wouldn't budge. Had he broken it? She buttoned the top and stretched her sweater downward to make herself decent.

For the first time since her orgasm, when he'd worn that beautiful little smile she'd thought so appealing, Nikolai met her gaze.

His was cold, distant, disgusted.

He stepped up to her and glared. When his eyes flickered to the door and back, she realized she was standing in front of it. He was waiting for her to move so he could leave.

Her face flamed hot and her heart thundered mortification through her veins. Biting her tongue to restrain the apology she almost uttered, Kate took three steps backward, clearing the door and putting lots of space between them.

Space he apparently wanted.

Nikolai reached through the bar and turned the key hanging in the lock. He pulled the door open and, without looking back, without another word, stalked out of the cell.

CHAPTER 8

Nikolai needed to punch something. Repeatedly. Anything to distract himself from the hurt and humiliation he'd seen in Katherine's pale blue eyes. The hurt and humiliation he'd put there.

What the hell had he been thinking?

He glared at Leo, standing with his arms crossed at the end of the hall, and dared the young warrior to give him a reason to lose his shit right here and now.

Leo dropped his gaze. "Anton's in the security booth."

The king—for it was the first time in a long time he felt so deadly serious about an order—got right up in the blond's face. "After the doc's done with her, you get her out of that cell. Back to Moscow. Out. Of. Here. We clear?"

"My lord—"

Nikolai fisted the man's T-shirt and dragged him in closer, flashing his fangs in warning. "Are we crystal fucking clear?"

Leo's gray eyes flared a silver light that hinted at the man's own building anger, but he kept his mouth closed.

"Nikolai," Mikhail said, stepping from the security booth. "Let him go."

He released Leo with a shove and stalked past his friend into the booth.

Anton dropped his phone into his pocket and smiled. "My lord, you're looking better. Want me to examine your n—"

"There's a human woman in there who got banged up earlier and was complaining of headaches." He pointed in the direction of the dungeons. "I want you to examine her. And then I want her out of here."

Anton shook his head, his good nature not dampened at all by Nikolai's lack of niceties. "I'm afraid that's not possible."

"Why the hell not?"

"Been snowing all day. Must be two feet of snow out there. Roads are a mess."

"You made it here okay."

"I made it as far as Poreche and hiked in the rest of the way until Leo rode out with the snowmobile. The roads back to Vasilievskoe are completely impassable."

Nikolai stared at him a long moment, then paced the room. He couldn't get rid of her.

Just perfect.

The weight of the other males' eyes settled on his shoulders like an anvil. He paused at the computer panel, his gaze falling on the controls to the security cameras. Heaving a breath, he hit a series of keys and buttons, bringing the monitor displaying the feed from Katherine's cell to life.

A pang his heart had no goddamn business feeling squeezed his chest.

She sat on the floor, in the exact spot he'd left her standing, her back against the bars and her arms hugging her legs in front of her. Her face rested sideways on her knees, so he couldn't make out her expression.

Damn it all to hell and back.

He wanted her.

He wanted more of the way he felt when he was around her. Lighter, freer, relieved just the smallest, life-giving amount from the constant suffocating press of his grief. She made him believe it was okay to take a breath, a single in and out of his lungs, without thinking of how he'd utterly failed his kid brothers.

And damn, she was so strong.

Despite being locked behind dungeon bars, the first thing she'd asked was if *he* was okay. Her compassion overwhelmed him again and again. He kept trying to imagine the scene Mikhail had earlier described. Her, feeding him and holding his warriors at gunpoint at the same time…

Of course, his men were there for him, but to think he'd met a woman with the mettle to do what she'd done, to stand up for him in a do-or-die situation. He wanted to melt into her, to crawl into his bed with her in his arms, to lay his head on her chest and sleep his pain away.

She was his equal, in every way. No, not true at all. She was so much better than him.

Yeah, and that kind of woman would never want a male so grossly tainted by dishonor.

He dragged his hand through his hair, and the movement of air carried her scent to his nose.

Jesus, she was fire wrapped in satin and silk.

She touched him, and he burned. But it hadn't been enough. With her, it would never be enough.

And that meant she had to go.

With the Soul Eaters so numerous they were nearly an infestation in Moscow, Saint Petersburg, Nizhny and Perm—not to mention the south of Russia, where cities like Saratov were actually losing population due to the evil ones' destructive addiction—he couldn't divide his attention enough to even consider a relationship.

That's a goddamn lie and you know it.

He could never have someone like Katherine Bordessa, and lose her. Simple as that. And the war was too volatile to chance it.

What a fucking coward he was. No hero material here, that was for sure.

He heaved a sigh. "Fine. Get her out of that damn cell, though. And get her some clean clothes."

With a final glance at the monitor, Nikolai offered a silent apology for the way he'd treated her, then turned his back on her image.

"You—" he glared at Leo "—sparring ring, ten minutes."

Voices echoed down the stone hall, but Kate couldn't really make them out. Well, not since Nikolai had growled out his command to send her back to Moscow.

She thumped her fist against her forehead. Stupid, stupid, stupid. How had she been so stupid?

Man, she'd heard of vampires' allure, how everything

around them felt so much more intense. And now she understood it firsthand. He'd made her believe he liked her, cared for her, wanted her. The reverence in his gaze as he healed her arm, the deep rasp of need in his voice as he encouraged her pleasure, the pet names that seemed to communicate affection and familiarity—she'd fallen for every last bit of it.

Worse, she'd thought it all *meant* something. As if.

She thunked her head against the bars behind her and immediately regretted it. The medicine Nikolai had brought had dimmed the ache, but the bump on the back of her head was still sore.

Wrong path, my butt. Leaving the service of the Proffered was the smartest thing she'd ever done. Tonight confirmed it once and for all.

Then why does it hurt so much?

Footsteps approached, diverting Kate's attention from her self-reflection.

Mikhail pushed through the still-open door and looked down at her with those analytical dark brown eyes. Another man entered behind him, thin and kind-faced. "Katherine, I understand Nikolai talked with you about seeing Anton, our doctor." He gestured to the other man, who smiled and nodded. "So, I'll leave you—"

"No."

Mikhail tilted his head. "I don't—"

"I won't see your doctor." She pushed up off the floor, grinding her teeth against the ache in her head.

"Nikolai said you were complaining of a headache after some sort of injury." Anton said in a calm, even voice. "Can you tell me what happened?"

"Skull versus frozen ground. Okay? I'm fine." She glanced at the man, then back to Mikhail, hating her rudeness but needing desperately to leave from where she wasn't wanted. "I know he wants me gone, so just give me my things and I'll be on my way."

Anton raised his hands. "The king was very clear," Anton said, apparently leaving it to Mikhail to decide. "He wants me to give her a clean bill of health, but I can't examine her against her will. I won't."

The doctor's words faded out as her brain focused on the first two that had so casually fallen from his lips.

The king.

Who was he talking about—

Oh, God, no. No, it can't be. No braid. No jewels. How can he be the king?

"He hasn't worn them in a while," Mikhail said.

"What?" Kate asked, the room doing that spinny thing again.

"I said he hasn't worn them in a while."

Oh, jeez, had she been thinking out loud?

Hoping to hide the blush heating her cheeks, Kate scrubbed her hands over her face, torn by conflicting desires: to know more, to know why Nikolai, the Vampire Warrior King of Russia, apparently, didn't wear the symbols of his rank and title, *and* to get the hell out of here. Now.

Because it wasn't just any old beautiful, sexy vampire who didn't want her. It was the freaking king.

Shit. What if word of this got back to her parents?

Nikolai seemed so disgusted with her when he left. They had her passport and cell phone. Surely it wouldn't take that much research on the vampires' part to determine her family's association with the Electorate Council. Bordessa wasn't that common a name.

As if a man being repulsed by bringing her to orgasm wasn't bad enough.

Anton broke the awkward silence. "Well, if you change your mind, just have someone come get me. It's not like we're going anywhere any time soon."

Kate frowned. "What's that supposed to mean?"

"Go ahead, Anton. I'll get you if we need you," Mikhail interjected. The man nodded and left. "It's snowing, Katherine. Heavily. The roads are closed."

She groaned, and her stomach dropped to the floor. "Tell me you're not serious."

"I'm afraid so." He sighed. "Look, I know you don't want to be here, but if you'll let me, I'd like to show you to a room where you'll at least be more comfortable."

"Why?"

"Because there's no need for you to be imprisoned. I'm sorry we did that in the first place."

Kate hugged herself and shrugged. What the hell. A real room would be nice, especially if it was near a bathroom. Or a shower. "Okay."

He held out his hand. "After you."

Without a backward glance, she stepped out of the cell.

"If you'll follow me," Mikhail said.

Down the stone hall, through some sort of empty high-tech office, Kate followed the warrior. The hallways leading through the downstairs were dark, rough-hewn, and she was fascinated despite herself. Wherever she was, this place was old. How she wished she could explore.

They came to a flight of wide stone steps and made their

way up. On the top landing, Mikhail entered a code into a pad on the wall, releasing the heavy door in front of them with a metallic click.

In contrast to the dim lighting of the lower level, this floor was all white-painted cinder blocks. The bright light revealed midnight-blue tones in Mikhail's jet hair. Along the long corridor, most of the doors were solid with only a single small square window at the top, so Kate could only get the most cursory of glances into her surroundings. In the distance, music with a driving bass beat caught her attention. The farther up the hall they walked, the louder it got.

A warrior—the young one who had manhandled her out in that parking lot—rounded a corner and made for the closest door. His gaze scanned down the front of her before meeting her eyes, and she couldn't read his expression. He pushed a door open, letting the screaming guitars and pounding drums blare out into the hallway full force.

"You're late," someone shouted from within.

"I'm still in time to kick your ass. *My lord.*"

Kate and Mikhail walked past the door as it eased shut. Through the narrow gap, Kate had just enough time to see Nikolai's shirtless broad back, the cut muscles decorated with more beautiful designs she couldn't fully make out.

His gaze cranked in her direction and their eyes met in the split second before the door closed between them.

God, every time she saw him, he was more gorgeous than the last.

Butterflies took flight in her stomach. "He's a warrior," she said, eyeing Mikhail's braid and trying to engage him for the first time since they'd departed her cell.

"Yes. A great one."

"Then, why no braid?"

"It's not my story to tell, Katherine." He started up a second set of stairs. "This way."

At the top, there was another keypad, and then they stepped into a modern-looking vestibule. When the door they'd come through clicked shut behind them, another door sprang open ahead of them. The room on the other side was like a huge family room. Massive leather sectional sofa, several leather recliners. A screen for a projection television. Behind a pool table sat several pinball machines, and a carved wooden bar lined a far wall.

She chuckled, taking in the liquor and beer bottles and empty glasses on the coffee and end tables. "Is this the vampire man cave?"

The side of Mikhail's mouth quirked up.

She shrugged. "My dad has a room like this. My mom calls it his man cave."

Mikhail smiled, just revealing the tips of his fangs. "I suppose so. We half live in this room."

For some reason, his smile made her sad. "None of you do that very often, you know that?"

"Do what?"

"Smile."

The jovial expression dropped from his face. "Not been a lot to smile about lately."

"I'm sorry to hear that."

He shook his head. "Just through here, then up one more flight."

Kate didn't fight him on the change of topic, and followed him out of the den. A central staircase came down to a wide foyer, flanked on the far side by a set of ornate doors with medieval Cyrillic characters in gold leaf forming an arch over the top.

Mikhail continued up the steps, but Kate hung back at the bottom, admiring the incredible painting all around the doors. "What's this room?" she asked, drawn to inspect the artwork more closely. When he didn't answer, she glanced over her shoulder.

He stood in the middle of the steps staring at her. "It is the Hall of the Grand Princes."

"Oh," Kate said, stepping back from the wall. She didn't know exactly what that was, but by the room's name and the tone of Mikhail's voice, she knew it was important.

An image sprang to mind, of Nikolai—King Nikolai, apparently—standing on a dais wearing a rich robe and gold crown. She didn't know whether to be amused or awed by the thought. "It's very beautiful."

He cleared his throat. "Thank you."

This time, when he turned, she followed him up the stairs. At the top, the decor changed yet again. Arched doorways, exposed buttresses in the ornate foyer, a tarnished but still striking cut-glass chandelier all framed lush carpets, vibrant wall tapestries and thick, heavy curtains covering the windows. Antiques sat chockablock to one another, and portraiture and other framed art vied for space on the crowded walls. The color scheme was rich and masculine—deep reds and dark blues, and appealed to her very much.

After several turns down a twisting hallway, Mikhail stopped outside a door. "This is one of the sixteen bedrooms in the house." He turned the brass knob and pushed into the dark, crossing the room to turn on a lamp next to a wide sleigh bed. "There's a bathroom through that door. I hope this will serve."

"It's great. Thank you." Her words were a complete understatement—the room was stunning, with wallpaper that gave her the impression of sitting amidst a great garden. But now that they were here, she didn't really want to be alone. It wasn't as if she could ask him to keep her company, though.

He scratched his jaw and said, "I will try to find you some clothing."

"Right. Thanks."

"Okay, then." He left, pulling the door shut behind him.

Kate released a long breath. This was the most surreal freaking night of her life. Or, wait, the most surreal *two* nights, she guessed.

After a quick trip to the bathroom, she poked around the large space, finally making her way to one of the windows. It took a minute to dig through the layer upon layer of heavy velvet curtains to finally get to the glass. Her efforts were rewarded with a ledge so wide she could sit on it.

Half sitting, she gazed out at the winter night, snow falling in a silent blanket on the dense forest. There was no view, really, but that didn't keep it from being beautiful, peaceful. She sighed.

She wasn't sure how long she'd been resting there when a knock sounded at the door. Wading through the miles of fabric made her laugh, and she was still grinning when she found Mikhail standing in the hallway with a thick stack of clothing in his hands.

"This is all going to be too big on you, so I brought several things for you to choose from."

Kate reached out for the pile.

Mikhail gaped. "Your arm." The tattered ends of her sleeve hung loose, revealing the smooth, unbroken surface of her skin. "He healed you?"

Heat exploded over Kate's face. She pulled the pile from his arms and hugged it against her chest. "I'm sure something will work. Thank you, Mikhail."

He stood there at loose ends, eyes wide, clearly wanting something else but not saying what it was.

She gestured at the clothes. "Well, thanks again."

His shoulders sagged. "Katherine?"

The hair rose on her arms and neck. "Yes?"

"Thank you for saving him. He's been my best friend for over five hundred years. I would've...well, we all would've been lost without him."

Five hundred years? The idea of it made her light-headed. She shook off the sensation. "Anyone would've—"

"No. What you did was special, and I stand indebted to you."

She watched him retreat down the hallway, looking every bit the warrior he was.

Kate turned again to the empty room, her hands trembling. Ridiculously, part of her felt so comfortable here, as if she belonged, and already felt the heartache of leaving them, of never seeing any of them again.

Never seeing Nikolai again.

CHAPTER 9

Nikolai bumped fists with Leo and gave him a shove. "Good match."

He chuckled. "You weren't half bad, for an old man."

The king barked out a laugh, the fighting having beaten some of the raging frustration out of him. "Says the two-hundred-and-twelve-year-old vampire."

He flashed Nikolai a grin.

"Thanks for sparring, Leo," he called as he reached the door.

"Yeah. Hey, my lord?" Twisting his shirt in his hands, Leo looked to the floor. "I didn't mean to, but I hurt her. I knocked her to the ground too roughly, and she hit her head."

Stomach clenching, heart pounding, Nikolai didn't need to ask which "her" he was referring to. "Why are you telling me this?"

Leo lifted his gaze and met Nikolai's head-on. "She really fought for you. Even got off a shot before I could disarm her.

I've never seen anything like it. Well, except for mated—" He clamped his mouth shut. "Just thought you should know."

Nikolai turned and wrenched the door open.

"Nikolai?"

Red flags waving in his mind, he froze but didn't look back.

"I see the way you look at her. They would want you to be happy."

He bolted from the room. No way he was having that conversation. Didn't matter that Leo had been Kyril's best friend—the two had been thick as goddamn thieves. Didn't matter that he meant well. It only mattered that he got the hell out of there, away from that wary look on Leo's face.

Away from his encouragements that he go after something he could never have.

Down the hall, up two staircases, through the meandering turns of the main floor. He knew the house like the inside of his own mind, and could've navigated it blindfolded, which was good since all he could see was *that look* on Katherine's face. As if he'd slapped her.

Well, hadn't he? No doubt the coldness in his words and actions had stung just as much.

He pressed his hand into the ache that settled under the bare skin of his chest.

Nikolai turned the corner into the wing that housed his private quarters, a series of rooms that formed a virtual apartment. His brothers' rooms had been in this part of Vasilievskoe, too, and their deaths had left the Vasilyev wing particularly still and quiet except for his own movements. Which was just fine by him.

Except…

Nearby, the plumbing whined. Someone was running the water. He backtracked and turned down an adjacent hallway. Light shined from under the door of the lone guest room in this part of the manor.

He was going to kill Mikhail.

Before he even thought to do it, he found himself standing in front of that door. *Her* door.

Oh, what the hell was he doing?

He should apologize. Rationale squarely in place, he rapped his knuckles against the heavy panel of wood. Then again. No answer. His gut clenched. Was that fucking worry he felt? "Katherine?"

He knocked his head against the door. Deep need rose within him, to lay eyes on her and reassure himself she was okay. She'd been attacked, bitten, kidnapped, and imprisoned. Not goddamn likely she was okay.

And that wasn't even considering what had happened between them, which had been phenomenal until he acted like a son of a bitch. The urge to see her made it hard to breathe.

He pushed through the door and called her name again. Two things struck him simultaneously: soft splashes of water from the direction of the open bathroom door and a stack of clothes on her bed.

Inside the room, her sweet-blooded scent infused the air and reawakened his cock, reminding him of his unsated arousal from before. Each breath pulled more of her into him, until he ached to penetrate her in return.

In any way she'd allow. In every way she'd allow.

Prickles on the skin of his right palm made him fist his hand.

His breath coming faster, shallower, Nikolai stepped over her discarded clothing to the bed and quickly flipped through the pile of fabric—robe, T-shirt, sweatshirt, sweatpants.

All Mikhail's.

An image flashed into his mind. Katherine, wearing Mikhail's shirt and sweatpants, so big on her she had to roll them at the waist and ankles. Katherine, wearing *Mikhail's* clothes.

Another. Male's. Clothes.

Nearly blind with a possessiveness he had no right to feel, Nikolai grabbed all the clothes and stalked out of the room. Bursting through the door to his apartment, he chucked everything in the general direction of the nearest trash can. He whipped his robe off the back of his closet door and ripped a few articles of clothing from a drawer. He wasn't even aware he'd returned to the guest room until her scent invaded his brain.

Nikolai glanced up, and found himself looking into Katherine's startled pale blue eyes.

"What are you doing?" Kate asked as she clutched the plush white towel tighter against her breasts. Her heart took off at a sprint as she drank him in. He radiated a dark energy that wrapped around her and resurrected that maddening ache in her left hand.

Maybe something wasn't fully healed after all.

"I brought you clothes," he nearly growled.

Kate glanced to the empty bed and pointed with the hand not holding the towel closed. "I had clothes."

Light flashed through the sapphire and his jaw ticked. "Those didn't work."

Staring at him, she tried to make sense of his completely confusing pronouncements. Which was hard when Kate couldn't help but notice the prominent bulge filling up the front of his workout gear.

Good God.

She hadn't finished toweling dry, but there was really no pretending that the slick wetness suddenly between her legs was from the bath. She shook her head. "How can clothes not work? Mikhail just brought them for me."

He growled. Literally growled.

She blinked and found him standing right in front of her, the ball of wadded-up clothing the only thing separating them. She gasped, breathing in the mouthwatering scent of his male spice, and stepped back.

Nikolai followed, kept pace with her as she retreated until she was trapped between him and the bed. "*His* clothes don't work. *His* clothes will *never* work."

Damn it, her left hand tingled as if it had fallen asleep. She shook it, and Nikolai's eyes tracked the movement. His tongue rubbed against the tip of a fang. Kate swallowed as she watched the sinuous movement of his pink tongue. She clenched her thighs, a tormenting throb blooming deep in her pussy.

"What do you want?" When he didn't answer, she braced herself and looked him in the eye.

"I want..." He turned on his heel and crossed to the door.

Brilliant, white-hot anger pounded through her veins. Every muscle strung tight, she leaned back against the bed. Not a chance in hell she was chasing after him, not again. No matter how much her body screamed for him to stay, for him to crawl on top of her and claim her as his.

No way.

In the silence between them, a tiny click sounded out. Despite herself, Kate glanced through the hanging threads of her damp hair to see him standing at the door. He dropped his hand from the lock.

For a moment, his stillness allowed her to study the ancient Cyrillic letters that spelled out two male names across his mountainous shoulders.

Then he tossed the clothes he'd been carrying to the floor. With leonine grace, he stalked back to her, his eyes boring into hers. Her body screamed in victory, more of that tantalizing moisture gathering on the sensitive lips of her pussy. She narrowed her eyes at him and arched a brow.

In front of her again, he stroked his knuckles over the hand holding the towel. Once, twice. Her nervous system sprang to life and set her to trembling.

He dragged his gaze from their hands to her eyes. "I want you, Kate. I shouldn't, because my head's a fucking mess. And I don't deserve you, after what I did to you before. But none of that changes the fact that I can think of *nothing* besides the idea of having just one perfect night. With you."

Kate shook her head. "You don't want me."

Light flashed in a wave behind his blue eyes. "I *do* want

you. I ache for you." He pushed his hips into her thigh, grinding his cock against her.

Kate couldn't seem to get enough oxygen into her lungs to clear her head. "That's not what you said," she whispered, almost gasping from the muscle spasm that rocked through her core.

He tilted his head and frowned. "You heard me?"

"Kinda hard not to."

The muscles in his jaw clenched. "I'm sorry. I was pissed at myself. Not at you. You, Katherine, you deserve only the best. And that's not me."

"Then why are you doing this?"

He licked his lips, flashing the tips of his fangs again. "Because, God help me, I am driven to distraction by the very thought of you." He cupped her face and caressed his thumb over her cheekbone. "By your beauty, by the fire in those lovely pale eyes." Stepping in closer, he bought them into contact from ankle to breast. "I am humbled by your compassion, proud beyond measure of your courage." He leaned his face into hers so that his breath tickled her lips. "I want you on my skin, in my mouth." He feathered his fingers down her bare arm, sending her into a shiver. "I want to see you naked, explore you with my hands, part your knees and bury myself in you. I want to hear you scream my name as I stroke deep and hard inside you. That's what I want."

Nikolai's unbridled honesty struck her like a match.

A flame roared up inside Kate, melting the reserve she'd built up after what happened earlier, making her body crave his so intensely she hurt. Tentatively, a part of her afraid he'd change his mind again, she reached out and weaved her fingers into his silky brown hair, where his braid should be. "But you're the king."

He leaned into her touch. "I'm just a male, like any male."

It was such a lie.

No man had ever turned the blood in her veins into flowing lava. No man had ever made her ache. No man had ever made her feel this…*alive*. It was all so overwhelming—she just had no experience feeling the things she felt, wanting the things she wanted. And he should know.

Taking a deep breath, she said, "I've never done this before, Nikolai." As her cheeks heated, she watched her fingers drag through his hair. Oh, he was so beautiful.

He tilted his head to force her to look at him. "Done what?" A range of expressions played out across his face. "You mean…" His eyes went wide. "Are you saying you're a virgin?"

CHAPTER 10

Heart triple-timing in his chest, Nikolai soaked in the beautiful flush on Katherine's cheeks and waited for her answer.

What had he ever done to find someone like her? Someone so beautiful, so strong, so damn perfect in every way.

For him.

She nodded, her eyes flickering to his and away again.

And Nikolai's thinking brain went offline.

Triumphant euphoria flooded into every cell. He locked his hands behind her neck and pulled her in for a kiss so deep, so intense, it drove everything else from his mind. His tongue explored her mouth, his hands massaged her neck and tugged her hair. Needing to be closer, to drive away every molecule of air separating them, he pushed between her legs and ground himself against her mound. Kate cried out and threw her head back.

"Oh, God, angel," he rasped. Her body was like a feast spread out before a starving man. And having denied himself the pleasure of a woman all these long months, he was exactly that. His lips fell to her throat, kissing, sucking, drawing the heated flavor of her skin onto his tongue. He laved long strokes against the throbbing pulse of her jugular, reveling in the drag of his fangs against her tender flesh. Jesus, he wanted to devour her. "I want you so damn much."

He scooped his hands under her thighs and lifted her atop the high bed. She wrapped her legs around his hips and her heels dug into his ass. He rocked his cock against her pussy, fascinated as the towel parted and rode up, inch by tantalizing inch.

Light fingertips fell on his bare chest and traced down the center of him, over the lines of his tattoo, making his stomach muscles flinch and clench. At the waistband of his pants, she stopped. Nikolai nearly groaned in need, but he didn't want to push her.

He wanted her to want him in return, so he had to let her go at her own pace.

His brain refused to let him think through everything that her still being a virgin could mean.

After the briefest hesitation, Kate's hand slid between them and gripped his cock over the thick cotton. That time, Nikolai couldn't restrain the groan the incredible contact drew out of him. "Christ, how you make me feel…"

His words seemed to encourage and embolden her. She massaged and squeezed, until he couldn't help but thrust into her hand.

Nikolai rubbed his fingers over the knuckles still clenching the towel in front of her breasts. "Katya, let me see you. Let go."

Those beautiful pale blue eyes gazing into his, she dropped her hand, and the towel slipped behind her.

Pressing his palm to the valley between her full breasts, Nikolai held Katherine's heavy-lidded gaze and counted the rapid thumps of her heart. Vitality thrummed through her and into him, tempted parts of his soul back to life he thought long gone. Dragging his hand down her body, over the curve of her belly and into the soft brown hair between her legs, Nikolai watched her watch him.

"What do *you* want, Katya?"

A deep blush roared over the flush already staining her cheeks. He leaned over her and rubbed his nose along her jaw. The blush strengthened the scent of her blood on the air. "You are so lovely. I have to know what you want."

She ducked her head against his. "I don't have the words," she answered. "I just want you."

Her words eased the ache in the center of his chest. Oh, what was she doing to him? With slow, gentle thrusts, he rolled his cock against the nerves at the top of her pussy.

"You don't know the words," he asked, "or it's hard to say them?"

"Oh, my God," she whispered. "Nikolai."

The desperation in her voice rocketed into his balls. Cupping her breasts, flicking her nipples with his thumbs, he nipped his fangs down the long column of her graceful neck.

"Tell me," he rasped.

Her throat worked at a rough swallow under his worshipful lips. Hoping to deaden the hot ache in his palm, he lowered his right hand to the wet lips of her pussy and rubbed slow, tight circles.

She released a high-pitched cry. "I need you," she whined.

"My what? My fingers?" He eased his middle and ring fingers into the depths of her core. His fingertips found the swollen glands he hoped would give her pleasure and massaged, reveling in the new flow of moisture over his palm. He breathed the scent of her arousal into his very soul.

Starting slow, he rocked his hand up and down. Her whimpers and gasps spurred him on. He fingered her faster, making sure the heel of his hand rubbed her clit, until the wetness of her juices around his moving fingers formed a raw, decadent sound track.

"Is this what you want?" he bit out as the walls of her pussy tightened.

"Yes," she cried. "No. No, I want…"

"What? Say it, angel."

"I want you to…oh, my God, Nikolai…I want you to f-fuck me. I want you inside me."

Damn it all to hell, this shy innocence together with what he knew of her courage and bravery was a combination so appealing, so arousing, it nearly took him to his knees. Bracing himself on the mattress beside her, he pumped his hand faster, harder, willing her body to let go.

The velvet walls of her pussy clamped down on his fingers. Katherine screamed and went boneless, falling back against the bed. He stroked her through the orgasm, milking out every last ounce of pleasure for her.

Katherine lifted her head, her eyes coming back into focus, and licked her lips. Her toes curled into the waistband of his pants. "Off."

"Yeah?" He pushed them to the floor, then crawled onto the bed between her knees. Hands under her hips, he guided her body higher on the mattress. A small soft palm wrapped around his cock. "Fuck," he said, surprised and pleased by her firm, sure grip.

Goddammit, he needed in her.

He *wanted* in her. Hand aching, fangs throbbing, dick leaking in her grasp, Nikolai stared wide-eyed at the incredible site of her jacking him off.

He was about to cross some cosmic line.

He knew it. He felt it in his gut.

But he couldn't pull back, couldn't resist the incredible seductiveness of Katherine Bordessa. He pulled her hand away and brought it to his mouth for a long kiss on her palm. That she smelled of his maleness caused his cock to twitch against his stomach.

"Katya, there's something you need to know about what is going to happen between us."

She tilted her head against the mattress, strands of her chocolate hair spread in a dark halo across the plush comforter, and stared at him a long minute. "You're going to bite me."

Hands braced on either side of her shoulders, he leaned over her. "How did you know that's what I was going to say?"

She arched an eyebrow. "Well, number one, you're a vampire."

Biting back a laugh, he arched a brow right back. "Fair point. And number two?"

"Nikolai, I trained as a Proffered."

"You...what?" His brain was so scattered he couldn't

pull his thoughts together to respond, to absorb the significance of her revelation. On top of everything, she was a Proffered? Groomed to be a vampire's mate? Emotion barreled through his veins—that dark rage from before reemerged at the thought he might've lost her to another, soul-deep gratitude warmed his chest as each new evidence of her rightness for him filled his heart, convinced his brain. All this, it felt so much bigger than him—magical and fated, even. "But you didn't serve?" he finally managed to say.

"I…no." She shook her head. "The whole thing scared me. I don't know."

"And now?"

"Now—" she released a shaky sigh "—I want you to bite me so damn bad I can barely lie still."

His heart was a freight train in his chest. How had he gone from nearly dying to having a chance to live again in just a few short hours.

Because of Katherine.

"Come here," she whispered, cupping his face in her hands. The touch was so gentle, the voice so sweet, she lured him in as surely as if magnets resided in the center of their chests. "Before, it was an abstraction. Now, it's just you. And, everything else aside, I want you, Nikolai." She lifted her hips and rubbed herself against him.

"Jesus," he said, taking his dick in hand. He was so hard, so sensitive, his own touch was nearly painful. "It may hurt, Katya, for a moment, but I will make it go away. Yes?"

She nodded. "I need you in me, Nikolai. The emptiness hurts already."

"I will take care of you," he murmured, his heart making plans his brain hadn't yet approved. But, in that instant, none of that mattered. Her words beckoned him in, welcomed him home, seduced him to believe they could have a chance.

Kate moaned and dug her fingers into the muscles straining with leashed power all down his sides. The steel length of his erection pushed into her, filled her with a heavy pressure that made her hold her breath.

"Angel, I can't——" He shook his head, blue eyes blazing, pleading.

She tugged at his back, urging him down. "Let go, Nikolai. I want it."

With a growl that ricocheted out of his throat and down her spine, Nikolai's weight covered her as he thrust forward, burying himself deep inside her in one hard stroke. Hunched around her, his hands curled under her shoulders and clasped tight. Kate cried out at the stretching invasion, but then his fangs sank into her throat, cutting off her voice.

His hips drew back and hammered home at the same time his tongue and teeth sucked a long, hot draw from her veins. The friction and the rush of blood worked together, easing her, melting her, making her hot, tense, and needy all over again.

Inhaling precious air, Kate surrendered to the dark ecstasy brewing between them. As soon as she did, arousal reignited within her body, erasing every care that didn't involve pleasing him over and over.

Her body was on fire, but her mind was calm. All the

angst, all the restlessness, all the questioning—it disappeared the moment they became one.

She buried her hands in his hair and cradled him against her throat. "Take me...take all you need," she said. He was so thick, so long, and filled her so perfectly, like a missing piece of her very soul she'd searched her whole life for and finally, miraculously, found.

As he fed from her vein, her palm erupted in a new sensation. An ache, to be sure, but this time, it was the burn of a need nearly fulfilled. Any discomfort that remained resulted solely from the incompleteness of her relief. She had no idea what any of this meant, but she knew it the way she knew she needed oxygen, or water. That was how she needed Nikolai.

So good, Katya, so good, so good. I can't get enough.

She gasped and awe-filled joy brought tears to her eyes. She could hear him again. The way she'd heard him out on that street.

Emotions welled up within her chest and seemed to rework the very DNA in her cells. Intense affection barreled through her veins until she was certain he must taste what she felt for him, what she would always feel for him, no matter what. Electricity spiraled through her and settled low in her belly, building, charging, threatening an explosive release she didn't think her body could possibly handle.

Stroke after delicious stroke brought his pelvis against her clit. She chased the maddening friction, lifting her hips, meeting his thrusts. Everywhere she reached out, her hands found hot, hard-bodied male flesh. Each breath sucked that incredible male spice—stronger and more attracting than she'd ever smelled it before—into her lungs until her toes curled against the bedding.

Forgive me, brothers. Wanting her doesn't mean I've forgotten you.

The desperate lamentation of his thoughts was so different from her own ecstatic pleasure, the pain behind the words urged a single tear to spill from her eye.

"Oh, Nikolai," she whispered through a tight throat, her hands stroking his hair. His words confused her—what had happened to his brothers? And were those the names on his back? But that didn't stop her protectiveness over him from rearing its head. "It's okay. You're okay. I've got you."

A strangled moan rang out of him. His fangs withdrew. He laved that healing tingle over his bite before lifting his gaze and meeting her eyes. The sapphire burned with emotion.

Kate cupped his face. "I can hear you," she whispered. "I don't know how, but I could out there in that alley, and I can now."

He opened his mouth to speak, and Kate's eyes went wide.

Dark red ringed his lips, coated his tongue.

A demanding, foreign hunger erupted in Kate's gut. She arched up, her mouth crashing into his, and sucked his tongue hard and deep, driven by a relentless need she'd never before experienced.

Kissing him wasn't enough.

She shoved at his shoulders, and he let her flip them over. Kate's hips took over their frantic dance, rising and falling over his cock, sucking him deep inside again and again. His big hands gripped her ass, grinding her down and lifting her back up. Her body was poised on the edge of a cliff, ready to fly to the heavens, to free-fall into space.

She just needed more of that red.

Clutching the hard angle of his jaws, Kate kissed him, sucked at him, whined that it wasn't enough. "What's happening to me?"

"Jesus, Katherine, talk to me."

She moaned against his lips. "I don't know, I don't know." Around the parched tightening of her throat, she swallowed, trying to ease the urgent thirst making her nearly insane. "Oh, my God, Nikolai. I want…I feel…"

His hands dug into her hair and forced their gazes to meet. "What, my sweet angel?"

"I want…your blood," she said so quietly she barely heard the confession leave her own lips.

Within her clenching cunt, Nikolai's cock grew harder, thicker. "Fuuuck, Katya, I think you are…." His words died in a groan as he rolled them in a messy tangle of limbs. Her head ended up right on the edge of the bed. "Oh, please," he begged, "if there's a God above."

With a roar, her king buried his fangs into the yielding flesh of her breast and erupted within her, igniting her own spasming release. His hips jerked and pressed as his mouth sucked her boneless.

It was the most glorious, peaceful, contented moment of her life.

She had nothing to compare the experience to, of course, but she already knew nothing would ever compare to Nikolai. He'd proven himself a giving and passionate lover, and in a few short hours had turned everything she'd thought she known about herself on its head.

Their bodies calmed, their panting breaths the only sound in the room, Nikolai licked closed his bite on her breast and lifted his head to meet her gaze.

Out of nowhere, a starburst of tingles exploded where their bodies were still connected. The sensation raced through her, fast and foreign, and left her insides feeling like a puzzle put together all wrong.

Kate gasped and clutched to Nikolai, and only held her panic at bay by focusing on the sheer and utter joy reshaping her new lover's face.

CHAPTER 11

Nikolai threw back his head and shouted a warrior's cry of victory. Katherine screamed, the nails on her right hand digging marks into his back. He grasped her left, interlocking their fingers.

"Hold on, angel," he gritted out.

All at once, the sensation disappeared, and Nikolai's gaze cut to their joined hands.

Delicate black markings formed an overlapping pattern of endless square knots that wrapped around his right hand and continued onto her left. His heart expanded in his chest until he was sure it would burst.

For the love of all that was holy, he'd found his mate.

As he stared at the mating mark in awe and wonder, the dream he'd had upon waking after surgery came back in vivid detail.

On some level, he'd known.

Her blood in his veins had revealed the truth. No matter how much he'd fought the idea, tried to deny what he'd been feeling these last long hours, she was meant to be his. And he, hers.

"Nikolai, our hands," she whispered, eyes wide and beautiful as she lifted their hands and studied the marks. "Is that—"

"It's a mating mark, Katya, and the mark of a good mating, too. See how small the knot work is, how tight?" She nodded, her gaze meeting his before returning to their hands. "The blood magic between us is strong. It tells me things I already suspected, though I resisted them, and now I know for sure."

"And what's that?" she asked, dragging those baby blues away from their joined grasp.

"That you were meant for me. In every way, you are my equal. Hell, my better. I admire you greatly, Katya, and not just for saving my life. Me, my warriors, we put you in an impossible situation, one you handled with grace and courage. I hate that we met in this time of war and chaos in my world, and God does it scare me that you could get hurt. But there's also no denying that the mere idea of you standing by my side through the good and the bad of it makes it…all so damn much easier to bear."

He felt the truth of those words down deep, down into the dark places within him that had before so filled with grief and guilt.

Reaching out to stroke the hair off her face, he shifted, reminding him that he remained buried in her sweet pussy. Despite the incredible, mind-bending orgasm, his cock was still as hard as she was wet.

He rocked his pelvis, slow and gentle, and hummed his

approval when she released a small moan and lifted her hips to meet his.

"What happened to your brothers?" she asked, her voice so full of that compassion he already associated with her. "On your back, it's their names, isn't it?"

He nodded. "They were killed in a battle with the Soul Eaters. Six months ago. They walked into an ambush, were outnumbered, and I couldn't get to them in time."

She squeezed his hand. "Oh, Nikolai, I'm so sorry."

"Don't be. It was my fault, and I will never forgive myself."

She tilted her hips, just the littlest amount, and he couldn't remain still. The soft give-and-take of their actions, of this new round of soul-bearing lovemaking, provided as much comfort as pleasure.

"No, I don't believe that. How could it be your fault?"

He scoffed. "We call the part of the city where they died the meat grinder, because all the abandoned buildings provide nests for the Soul Eaters. We used to play poker to see who got that sector on patrol. Kyril and Evgeny died because I bluffed my way through a hand of seven-card straight."

Swallowing roughly, she dragged the fingers on her free hand through the left side of his hair. "Is that why you refuse to wear the marks of your position?"

"I dishonored myself, Katya. As a warrior, as a ruler, by playing games with men's lives, with the lives of my only living blooded relatives. I lost the right to call myself warrior, or king."

"Do you want to know what I think?"

He kissed her hand, still intertwined with his, and rocked his body into hers in an easy, gentle rhythm. "Always."

"I didn't know your brothers, of course, but I have brothers of my own. And though sometimes we want to kill each other, they have always been my greatest defenders, and the first ones to call me out when I acted like a brat. And I just think…I think your brothers wouldn't want you to turn your back on something so important, Nikolai. Kings rule. Warriors fight. That's who you are, and who you should be." She licked her lips and offered a small smile. "They wouldn't want you to stop living just because they no longer do."

Her words lodged a knot in his throat. Oh, God in heaven, he was falling in love with this woman.

"Will you tell me about them sometime?" she asked, wrapping an arm around him and pulling them closer together.

"Will you stay long enough to hear all there is to tell?"

She glanced at their hands and squeezed. "Is that what this means?" Her pale eyes went wide and a light blush colored her cheeks. "Oh, I guess I just assumed—"

"Shh, angel, yes, it's what it *can* mean. It's what I *want* it to mean." His heart tripped into a sprint. "The mark will last three days, then disappear forever if the mating is not consummated."

He rolled onto his side and pulled Katherine to him, holding her thigh open so he could maintain their intimate connection.

Even as his hips moved, he spoke words he never thought he would: "Will you be my mate, Katherine? Will you stand at my side, serve as my queen and share in my life, my blood, my immortality?" Now that he'd surrendered to the blood magic so clearly working between them, he felt the rightness of it down deep.

She gasped and grasped her throat, as if surprised. "Oh, Nikolai, are you sure? You said one night. Just one perfect night."

"Angel, I'm more than sure. I didn't dare hope for more than that. And, now...now that I have the chance for a lifetime of perfect nights, a chance at a lifetime with you, I want it more than anything I've ever wanted in my very long life."

She smiled. "I do want you, Nikolai. I truly do. I left the service of the Proffered and fled five thousand miles around the world to get away from it, I thought. But, really, something in me just knew that, had I stayed, I'd have been in the service of the wrong warrior. The wrong vampire. The wrong king. How fast this has all happened is crazy, but I want you, a life with you, all of it." She bit down on her bottom lip and one hand rubbed at her throat.

Her words were like the sweetest salve, knitting up the raw edges of the psychic wounds he bore deep within. But still, he frowned. Unease stirred in his gut. Something wasn't right... "Are you okay?" He grasped her hand before she marked her neck.

She trembled. Nodded. "I...I don't...I'm *so thirsty*, Nikolai."

The world went still around him. They weren't mated. Not yet. But every instinct told him she was hungry and hurting for the want of his blood.

Jesus. How could he make her wait until the ceremony

to feed? Even if they held it at tomorrow's nightfall, that was hours away.

He couldn't. He didn't want to.

An idea came to mind. Maybe he didn't have to, either.

Withdrawing from her body, he squeezed her hands. "I want to ease you, angel." He reached over the side of the bed and found his pants. From the pocket, he retrieved a small leather pouch. He returned to her and pulled the drawstring open. "Hold out your hand."

Four faceted gemstones and a few little bands poured out into her palm. She gasped and leaned in, turning her hand this way and that to catch the light of the stones.

He smiled, knowing just how fascinating they were to look at. "They're alexandrite. Our sacred stone. Very rare. It changes color in different lights." Just then, they appeared red with flashes of pale purple.

"Oh, they're beautiful. I've never seen anything like it. But, how will this help—"

"If you'll allow it, I would like to share a private consummation with you. Right here. Right now. I still want the formal ceremony, Katherine. I want to stand before you and my warriors and claim you as my own, but I can't watch you suffer, not when I can take the pain away."

"Oh, Nikolai, yes."

Deep satisfaction pooled in his gut. The thought of her feeding from *his* vein seduced him with the rightness of the plan. "But I need you to hold on a moment longer, if you can, because you deserve a male doing his duty, shouldering his responsibilities. And I want to be that kind of a male, for you. So—" he lay on his back next to her, his marked hand settling on his chest "—it doesn't have to be perfect, but if you could braid three of those into my hair…"

"You want *me* to do it?"

He looked at her and smiled. "Who else would I ask, my angel?"

"Okay," she whispered.

As her fingers grabbed and tugged thick strands of his hair, Nikolai closed his eyes and imagined all there was to come. Her mouth filled with the flavor of his blood. The consummation mark adding color to the black of their hands. Standing within a circle of his warriors and publicly claiming her, and being claimed in return.

A new blooded family. Maybe even a newling, someday.

She'd brought him back to life, and now she was giving him the world.

Trembling fingers stroked over his hair. "It's done," she said, voice tight with need. "What should I do with this one?" She held the last jewel between her fingers.

He drew her down for a single slow, deep kiss, then took the stone from her. "This one is going to bring you ease." Placing a faceted edge against the uninjured side of his throat, he pressed the jewel hard into his flesh until he felt the burn of the laceration, and then he scored a long line. Warm blood bloomed over his skin, pooled and ran down the side of his neck.

Her eyes went wide, her mouth dropped open. Her heartbeat thundered in the quiet of the room.

"What do you want, Katherine?" he said in a tight voice, his cock reawakening against his belly.

He didn't have to ask twice.

She fell over him, her mouth finding and licking the

crimson stream, her body writhing and shifting until she lay atop him.

Masculine satisfaction roared out of him, pounded through his dick, made his balls grow heavy with need. But this wasn't just about him.

Nothing would be, ever again. Thank God.

For, he was meant to serve. And while, by lineage and all that was just in the world, he had a duty to serve as king and commander, by choice he would also serve his mate, his angel, his…love.

Always and first, for however many nights he had left.

Her mouth sealed over the cut and sucked the lifeblood directly from his body. Five hundred years of living and fighting all came down to this moment, and he could wait no longer. Lifting his head, he struck his fangs into the soft tendon where neck met shoulder, and completed the bonded circle of blood between them.

The first swallow of her nectar brought her thoughts into his mind.

Oh, God, I love him I love him I love him.

The words reassembled him into a new male, a better male, *her male*, tonight and forever.

Feasting on her blood, and feeling the connection cycling through and between them, Nikolai thought in reply, *As I love you, Katherine. Now, take whatever you need, take everything, because we have all night, and I am yours. Forever.*

CHAPTER 12

FOUR MONTHS LATER...

Kate stood in the shooting booth, aimed her pistol at the target at the end of her firing lane, and squeezed off six quick shots.

A grin crept up her face.

Three in the head. Three in the heart.

And bonus that she didn't even have to reel the target in to see the details of her hits, because the combination of Nikolai's and their newling's blood in her system had given her remarkably improved eyesight.

If Nikolai had been protective of her after their consummation ceremony—well, after *both* of their ceremonies, one official with all the warriors present, and that first private one that was just for them—it was nothing compared to how protective he'd become since they realized she was pregnant with his son a month later. And while he did pamper and fuss over her sometimes, Nikolai was a warrior through and through and agreed that she ought to know how to defend herself—and their young—should she ever find herself having to do so.

After all, Kate had once had to defend Nikolai, which was the argument that finally convinced him this was a good idea.

Strong arms wrapped around her baby bump. "There you are," Nikolai said in her ear, his voice low and sexy.

"Hey. How did your meeting go?"

He unleashed a long breath. Nikolai had been bringing her up to speed on the state of the vampire world—and specifically on the state of the threat posed by the Soul Eaters. And the long and short of it was that the threat was growing, which was why the world's seven remaining vampire kings had a strategy meeting by teleconference that'd taken up the whole night and half the morning.

"As good as it could go. The good news is that our mating and that of Kael and Shayla in Northern Ireland has the Electorate Council more committed than ever to what we need from humankind." He pressed a kiss to her throat, one that spoke of needing comfort rather than wanting something of a more physical nature. "What are you doing down here?"

"Just practicing. Look at that. I'm getting good."

"Fuck good, angel. You're getting great. Remind me never to get on your bad side."

She threw her head back on a laugh, until she was resting against his broad shoulder. "You mean by, like, throwing me in your dungeon?"

He took the Sig from her grip and secured it, then urged her to turn to face him. "Not everything that happened in the dungeon was bad, was it, Katya? I still get hard remembering you up against the bars." A glow flashed from behind those sapphire eyes.

She felt the proof of his words growing against her belly. "Do you now?" she said, trying to play it like she was all nonchalant when she knew she was failing because him talking dirty and getting aroused made her aroused, which he had multiple ways of determining that she couldn't control—he could smell her arousal, see her eyes dilating, and hear her heart beat faster.

She really couldn't hide much from her vampire. Not that she wanted to.

"Mmhmm. Everything about you makes me hard."

Kate grinned, just feeling so damn happy. Every single thing that had happened since that winter night had been unexpected—and in some cases things she thought she *didn't* want—but standing here with the man, the vampire, the king she loved, she couldn't imagine her life any other way. Didn't want to imagine it, either. "Surely not everything."

Dark humor crept over his expression, and damn did he wear humor and happiness well. In the months since they'd met and mated, it was almost as if a weight had lifted off Nikolai. It wasn't that he wasn't still grieving his brothers, because he was and that might never stop, but everyday he was getting closer to being able to admit it wasn't his fault. And Kate was doing everything she could to make him believe he was lovable and worthy of being loved.

It all showed. On his handsome face. In the brightness of his eyes. In the straightness of his shoulders. In the way he joked and laughed with his brothers. And when she and Nikolai fed from each other, she could sense and feel his growing peace from inside the very heart of him. And she loved that for him.

She just…loved him.

"Yes, everything." He arched an eyebrow, affecting a stern countenance that was so freaking hot.

Grinning, Kate looked down between them. "Really? My growing belly?"

"Fuck, yes," he said, dropping to a knee, lifting her shirt, and pressing his lips to her stomach. "Knowing you carry our newling absolutely turns me on. You and our son give me hope and solace and make me so damn proud. I can't wait to hold him in a few months."

Kate placed her hands over where his rested on her sides. One of the weirdest things to get used to was the ways in which vampire pregnancies—and apparently vampire maturation—differed from that of humans. *Everything* was faster. Vampire pregnancies were just six months instead of humans' nine. And vampire young achieved the human equivalent of adult development by the annual age of twelve. So it was hard to believe she was already halfway through her pregnancy, and sometimes actually dizzying how fast her body was changing.

"I can't wait to see you with a little baby in your arms, either. You are going to be such a hot father—I mean *good* father!"

"A hot father, huh?"

"I meant good. Freudian slip." Her cheeks hurt an absolutely stupid amount from smiling so much.

"No way you're taking that back. And now the fact that you're going to think it's hot when I hold Kolya is something else that's going to make me hard. See?" He boxed her in tighter against the wall that separated the empaneled shooting booth from the firing lane and let her feel every hard inch of him.

Kolya. Short for Nikolai. Like father, like son. And she was completely and utterly okay with that.

She wrapped her arms around his neck. "*Fine*. I suppose you're a little hot."

He growled. Literally growled. And the sound ricocheted an urgent heat into her lower belly.

Nikolai let her see his fangs extend and then made slow, slow work of lowering his face to her throat. And then his bite penetrated her skin and claimed her. *Only a little?*, came her vampire's voice in her mind.

God, she loved the intimacy of their connection. And once she'd worried that a relationship with a vampire would be nothing more than convenient biology.

"I guess more than a little," she rasped, her thirst making its demands known as it always did, but even more so since she'd been pregnant. She was eating and drinking for two now, and the baby's accelerated growth meant she was always hungry. For food. For Nikolai. "No fair. I need you, too."

Do you now? He repeated her teasing words back to her. Damn him.

"Nikolai, please."

Just like that, he released her, licked the bite closed, and picked her up so that her legs went around his hips. She laughed at the surprising quickness of his movements and held on tight as he carried her out of Vasilievskoe's indoor gun range. And then up and up and up to their apartment.

But not before passing half the warriors.

From where he was working out in the gym, Leo sniggered when he saw them go past.

"Got something to say, Leo?" Nikolai called without stopping.

"Have fun, my lord." The gray-eyed vampire's tone was full of teasing.

"Oh, my God," Kate said, burying her face against Nikolai's cheek. He just chuckled.

In the warriors' vamp cave—re-nicknamed because they all objected to her calling it a *man* cave since they weren't men—they passed Mikhail and Anton where they sat drinking whiskey and watching a movie with lots of loud, fast cars. Nikolai had kept the doctor with them wherever they were in case Kate were to have any complications.

Formal as always, Mishka shot to his feet. "Everything all right, my lord, my lady?"

Kate still wasn't used to that—to being a freaking queen—but at least Mikhail was the only one who routinely insisted on referring to her new status outside of ceremonial occasions.

Nikolai spun in a circle and grinned. "Everything is fucking excellent."

Mikhail laughed. "Very good, my lord."

Kate looked over her shoulder as her king kept right on moving. "You vampires need to get mated soon because I need more estrogen in this place."

"Yeah," Nikolai called as he raced up the steps. "Consider that a royal order."

"Ooh, I could get used to giving orders." Kate laughed as Nikolai kicked their apartment door shut with his boot.

"Is that so?" he asked, those blue eyes flashing with all the heat he'd banked in the time it took them to get to their bedroom. He placed her down on their bed and leaned over her, forcing her to recline beneath him. "Do you have an order for me?"

Kate thought about it for a long moment, until a picture took shape in her mind and she gave voice to it. "Anything?"

"Anything, Katya. But tell me now because I'm not feeling very patient."

She let him see every bit of desire she felt in the way she looked at him as she spoke. "Undress us, put on your crown, and then get on your knees between mine."

The growl that rumbled in his throat was so freaking hot.

"And then?" he asked, already working off her jeans as he kicked off his boots.

"Put that sexy mouth on me." She arched a brow at him.

They both took care of their own shirts, and Kate shrugged out of her bra as she watched six-foot-five inches of devastatingly masculine vampire cross the room to retrieve his crown from its big velvet-lined box.

In mere seconds he was right where she'd told him to be. On his knees, pushing her knees apart, wearing a priceless, ancient gold crown at a rakish angle. He nailed her with a heated stare. "I am going to fucking devour you."

"I was counting on tha—" His actions stole her breath.

His mouth stole her sanity.

His heart had utterly stolen hers.

Because she was all the way seduced by her vampire king. And always would be.

Thank you for reading! I hope you loved meeting Nikolai and Kate. The next book in the Vampire Warrior Kings series is TAKEN BY THE VAMPIRE KING. Find out what happens when a dying vampire king rescues a woman—then takes her prisoner when he realizes she's the only one who can save him. If you're a Beauty and the Beast fan like I am, you're going to love Henrik and Kaira's love story!

> *"OH.MY.GOD. Laura Kaye delivers as only she knows how....The sensual tension is...h.o.t. and the love making is...*sigh* Laura Kaye's fans will fall in love yet again!"* ~In Love with Romance Blog

Reviews are so helpful to authors and other readers. Please leave reviews of this book on Goodreads and your preferred retailers' sites. Thank you!

Be first to know about new releases, sales, and cover art, or you'd enjoy exclusive giveaways and prizes, sign up for my newsletter: http://smarturl.it/subscribeLauraKaye

READ THE NEXT BOOK IN THE SERIES!

TAKEN BY THE VAMPIRE KING
CHAPTER 1

"I am dying," Henrik Magnusson said. "We all know it."

Standing at the head of the council table, he looked over the grim faces of his warriors, most of them suddenly fascinated by the three-hundred-year-old expanse of spruce in front of them. He didn't blame them for the avoidance. It was hard to stare mortality in the face, especially when your kind was supposed to be immortal.

"It's time to talk succession."

Jakob's gaze shot up, anger and resolution burning in his blue eyes. "It is not. My lord," he added as an afterthought. "We will bring in more Proffered."

Over the past decades, they'd brought in many virginal human women trained to serve the blood needs of the vampire warrior class to cure him. Not only had Henrik not

READ THE NEXT BOOK IN THE SERIES!

found a mate to sustain him, he'd never once blood-matched with any of the women. And their blood, at best, provided only a temporary alleviation of his inexplicably deteriorating condition. It had gotten to the point that he barely found blood palatable anymore.

"We will. But it will not likely work. My death is an eventuality for which we must plan."

Jakob shoved up from his chair. "I will not rest until we find the one who can..." *Save you.*

The words hung in the cool air and bounced between the gray, stone walls as if the warrior, Henrik's brother and the sole heir to the throne, had shouted them.

His brother shook his head and met the hard gaze of each of his brothers-in-arms. "We will not give up."

Murmurs of agreement rumbled through the room.

Henrik slammed his fist upon the table and flashed his fangs. "I. Am. Dying!"

The room and every vampire in it went preternaturally still. Jakob's expression was frozen somewhere between grief and rage.

Breathing hard, Henrik willed the tension from his shoulders. Human blood, especially from a mate, was a stabilizing force that guaranteed a vampire's immortality and humanity. But it had been a long time since Henrik's body had processed blood that way, so he'd steadily been losing both—and the past year had been the worst of all. When the rages came, he struggled to control them, and he was walking a very fine line right now.

Henrik stared at his brother a long moment.

The male appeared a much younger version of himself. He possessed the blond hair Henrik had before his mysterious ailment had turned it nearly white. And Jakob's eyes remained a dark, turbulent blue, like the color of the seawater that flowed through the many fjords snaking through their native Norwegian lands, while Henrik's had dulled to pale blue ice.

"Goddamnit." The king stalked away from the table and crossed to the uncovered windows along the far wall.

The polar night afforded them the luxury of leaving open this portal to the outside world. For three months each year, the sun never rose, turning the north lands into the perfect home for a vampire. But as with all things, the full darkness of Mørketid ended, bringing a month of Seinvinter, when daylight slowly returned in advance of the sun once again cresting the horizon.

Tomorrow was Soldagen, the first day of sunlight's return. The day marked the end of the last polar night Henrik would likely ever see.

He braced his hands against the ledge and stared up at the undulating lights in the night sky. Within the diffuse green of the aurora borealis was a sharp-edged curtain of rare—and ominous—red.

"Even the lights foretell my fate," he said, forcing calm into his voice.

He turned back to his warriors, every one of whom would've laid down his life for Henrik if they could. Jakob remained standing, stance ready, muscles braced. His dogged determination would make him a good king. And since only seven vampire warrior kings remained around the world, Henrik would do everything he could to ensure his brother ascended to the throne with the full support of these males.

READ THE NEXT BOOK IN THE SERIES!

"I require a vow from each of you. Follow and honor Jakob upon my death as you have followed and honored me these past four centuries."

For a long moment, no one reacted. And then Erik pushed up out of a chair.

Jakob's face went red, his fangs punching out. "Erik—"

The warrior held up a hand. "What my king asks of me I am more than willing to give." He crossed the room, met Henrik's gaze and sank to one knee.

Henrik held out the hand adorned with the ring that bore his family's royal crest.

Erik grasped his fingers. "I pledge my allegiance to Jakob Magnusson to ascend to the throne as Warrior King of the Northern Vampires upon the end of your reign. As a warrior, as a male of honor, I give my vow." Erik kissed the ring.

Henrik nodded as the warrior rose. One by one, the others followed suit. Lars, Kjell, Jens, Marius. Each gave Jakob an apologetic look before crossing the room and vowing to support him when the time came for his brother to die.

Their steadfast loyalty eased the turmoil that had become a constant presence in Henrik's veins. He couldn't control his mysterious malady, but this, *this* he could control. When he left this world for Valhalla, he wanted to know he'd done everything he could to leave his brethren strong and whole.

After all, the war with their ancient enemies, the Soul Eaters, would not cease just because he no longer lived to fight it.

When the last of them had given their vow, Henrik met

each of their gazes. "Thank you, old friends. Now, head out on patrol. The town fills with tourists for the festival and we must do as we've always done and stand ready to defend the humans against evil should the need arise."

The Soul Eaters—so named for stealing the souls of their human victims by draining them through the last stutter of their hearts—were equally attracted to night's reign in the north. And the influx of thousands of visitors for Tromsø's annual Nordlysfestivalen combined with the last days of darkness made the Soul Eaters even more brazen than usual.

The warriors filed out of the room, quiet and solemn.

All except Jakob, who remained in the exact same place since he'd stood to offer his protest. He braced his hands on his hips and shook his head, then slowly made his way around the table until he stood before his king. Tension rolled off the male in palpable waves. "You are giving up."

Malice shooting through his veins, Henrik got right in the younger vampire's face. "*Nei*, I am being realistic."

Jakob's blue eyes flashed. "Fuck realistic. Warriors *fight*." He jabbed his finger into Henrik's chest. "*You* have given up."

The king's fist was in motion before he'd even thought to respond. His brother's head snapped back as blood exploded from his lip. The sight further fueled the monster inside him, and Henrik struck again, unleashing a rib-snapping punch to Jakob's side. The warrior staggered but just managed to regain his footing before he fell. And still he didn't raise his hands in return.

"Fight back!" Henrik swung again, delivering an

uppercut to the jaw that slammed his brother against the stone wall.

"*Nei*," Jakob growled.

The next swing split open the warrior's cheek just below his eye.

"Fight back, damn you!"

Jakob held still against the wall. "Not until you do."

The words sank into Henrik's rational consciousness and gave him pause. He stumbled backward, one step, two, until he crashed into one of the chairs at the large table. And then the battle was all in his head between the two diverging sides of himself.

Between the monster and the man.

The former was getting stronger every day, no matter how hard the latter fought to rein it in.

He dropped his forehead into his hands and curled his fingers into fists in his hair. He was so *thirsty*.

Emptiness ached into the depths of his very soul. Every tissue in his body screamed for sustenance, but what was the use? Feeding brought him so little relief that the torment was greater after each failed attempt.

A hand gripped Henrik's shoulder.

"Fight, brother," Jakob said, his tone strained. "Stay with me and fight."

The king mulled over the words for a long moment, their wisdom sinking deep. No matter how desperate things looked, he had to hold it together. He had to fight. If for no other reason than to prevent Jakob and the others from being distracted out in the field by their worry for him. "All right."

"Yeah?"

READ THE NEXT BOOK IN THE SERIES!

Henrik nodded. "And I'm sorry." He jutted his chin toward the wall. "I'll fight. I'll fight this as long as I can. But you have to promise me something in return."

"Name it."

Henrik hated asking this of Jakob, of all people, but his brother was one of the few physically matched enough to heed the request.

"I'd rather be dead than a menace. When the day comes that I have lost all humanity, when all that remains is a monster in man's clothing, I want you to be the one to finish it."

Order TAKEN BY THE VAMPIRE KING Today!

ABOUT THE AUTHOR

Laura Kaye is the New York Times and USA Today best-selling author of over forty books in contemporary and erotic romance and romantic suspense. Laura grew up amidst family lore involving angels, ghosts, and evil-eye curses, cementing her life-long fascination with storytelling and the supernatural. Laura lives in Maryland with her husband and two daughters, and appreciates her view of the Chesapeake Bay every day.

Visit Laura Kaye at LauraKayeAuthor.com

Subscribe to Laura's Newsletter:
http://smarturl.it/subscribeLauraKaye

facebook.com/laurakayewrites
twitter.com/laurakayeauthor
instagram.com/laurakayeauthor

ALSO BY LAURA KAYE

Vampire Warrior Kings Series
IN THE SERVICE OF THE KING
SEDUCED BY THE VAMPIRE KING
TAKEN BY THE VAMPIRE KING

Want more vampires?
FOREVER FREED

Hard Ink Series
HARD AS IT GETS
HARD AS YOU CAN
HARD TO HOLD ON TO
HARD TO COME BY
HARD TO BE GOOD
HARD TO LET GO
HARD AS STEEL
HARD EVER AFTER
HARD TO SERVE

Warrior Fight Club Series
FIGHTING FOR EVERYTHING
FIGHTING FOR WHAT'S HIS
WORTH FIGHTING FOR
FIGHTING THE FIRE – COMING 2020

Blasphemy Series
HARD TO SERVE
BOUND TO SUBMIT
MASTERING HER SENSES
EYES ON YOU
THEIRS TO TAKE
ON HIS KNEES
SWITCHING FOR HER – COMING 2020

Raven Riders
RIDE HARD
RIDE ROUGH
RIDE WILD
RIDE DIRTY
RIDE DEEP – COMING 2020

Hearts in Darkness Duet
HEARTS IN DARKNESS
LOVE IN THE LIGHT

Heroes Series

HER FORBIDDEN HERO
ONE NIGHT WITH A HERO

Stand Alone Titles
DARE TO RESIST
JUST GOTTA SAY

Printed in Great Britain
by Amazon